DE-SEXED,

A Genderless World.

DE-SEXED,
A Genderless World.

BEN TARIRI

authorHOUSE®

AuthorHouse™
1663 Liberty Drive
Bloomington, IN 47403
www.authorhouse.com
Phone: 1 (800) 839-8640

Published by AuthorHouse 08/07/2019

ISBN: 978-1-4918-3729-0 (sc)
ISBN: 978-1-4918-3731-3 (hc)
ISBN: 978-1-4918-3730-6 (e)

Library of Congress Control Number: 2013920692

Print information available on the last page.

To: Cameron, Sammy, and Rod with love

DE-SEXED:

A Genderless

World.

ABOUT THE AUTHOR

Benjamin Tariri is a free-lance author in Boston, Massachusetts.
He has three sons, and lives with his family. Ben is also a
practicing attorney. He can be reached by
email at: INFO@DE-SEXED.COM

TABLE OF CONTENTS

DE-SEXED: A Genderless World.

Imagination will often carry us to worlds that never were.

But without it we go nowhere.

Carl Sagan

Dead bodies lay piled up on top of one another on the sidewalks. The corpses though look neatly arranged and well preserved. Like costume props in a high-school play, while their clothing appear old and dusty, they otherwise seem fresh without any signs of wear or decay. There is no sweet sickly stench of death anywhere. Yet, there are no signs of life, no birds, not even flies, except for an elderly couple on the sidewalk. The two huddle on a street corner, in front of a CVS pharmacy, its doors bolted shut with heavy chains.

The woman gasps for air, her grey hair partially covering a wrinkled face. Her ruby-colored velvet dress looks out of place, almost garish, sweat rolls down her high forehead as she opens and closes her deep blue eyes, as she tries to maintain her consciousness by looking to the man beside her. The man, tall and dressed in a superbly-tailored suit kneels down over her, holding her hands. The arch of his back makes him seem dignified, but yet helpless, even desperate. Both look wrung out. The woman opens her eyes again, lids lifted halfway, and as she surveys his face, he begins to weep. They seem to have years of understanding and harmony as they gaze at each other.

Her lips are cracked from dryness, and her voice trembles. "Please go darling. There's nothing that can be done. Leave. Don't stay for me."

"No! I can't let you suffer alone and I can't suffer without you," he says, his tears dripping onto her cheeks.

The man reaches in his pocket, and grabs hold of something. It is wrapped in a white handkerchief. He holds it in his palm, as he unwraps the fabric. It's an old revolver, a Big Ben Colt double barrel, circa 1940's. He sits down beside his wife, and holds her hand with his free hand. Tears stream down his red wrinkly face, and she gently wipes them away.

"It's alright my dear. It's alright," she says.

He says, "I love you too."

He then raises his other hand, points the cold barrel of the pistol at her, and presses the trigger. One shot only.

CHAPTER 1: *THE VISITORS*

The white Milky Way swirls amid a sea of galaxies, glowing and pulsating in scarlets and gold, emerald greens and whites. A dark blue light shimmers as it speeds towards Earth.

An older woman's voice announces, "A job well done people. We have returned. We will soon reclaim our homeland."

The cylindrical spaceship slows with a whooshing sound as it nears Earth's atmosphere, and soon it holds. Below, in streets, throngs of people move about in towns, cities and countries. A couple holds hands as they leave a Broadway show. A large group of all ages dance to the rhythm of Tai Chi in Shanghai. Zebras saunter and graze in African plains; butterflies dance with the breeze as they spiral above Mexican forests. Whales spout water in the cold Atlantic Ocean while dolphins frolic in the San Francisco bay.

A young man's excited voice says, "But I see life here still! Those are humans, aren't they? So many species. I even see insects and fish. Can we catch some? I want to study them!" He says in his boyish voice. "What are those yellow things in front of some buildings, look like the

3

letter M. Look at here, wow! big bowls full of people!" he exclaims, as he points to McDonalds restaurants and a sports stadium.

The elders ignore the young man, who is one of eight people seated around a sleek round table, the surface of which is a large monitor, with multiple moving views. This is Team 9, consisting of five males and four females, of varied ages, seemingly ordinary human beings, but without exception, all mentally superb.

Alex, a well-groomed grey-haired man, perhaps in his late sixties looks intently at the monitor, "Sadly, this is a problem. What to do with this mess? We can't re-inhabit in the middle of throngs of people, animals, fish, insects, even germs and bacteria. It's absurd, and actually impossible. We are already stretching our resources as is. We need every spot we can find on this planet."

"We can simply nuke them. We do have the nuclear weapons with us anyway. We even used nukes to propel us out of our own planet. But let me take some of the species to study first," says Andre, the same 20 something who had spoken earlier.

"No. We don't want to harm the Earth. We just need to rid it of its pestilence," says Alex. "And don't forget, some insects and single-cell beings are resistant to radioactivity, or may already be shielded from it."

"Let's freeze the atmosphere, which will destroy all forms of life." suggests Wang, a pretty, skinny young girl about Andre's age.

Elizabeth, a smart-looking, middle-aged woman with short blond

4

hair, says, "Let's not jump to decisions here. Remember, though we came at different times, we all originated from there." She points to the monitor." And we will feel right at home. But there's simply no room for more."

Maryam, speaking in a low, persuasive voice, turns to Wang and says, "My dear Wang, please consider the consequences. That would destroy the landscape, and might still not kill everything. Besides, we do not want to create a cemetery on Earth. Did we travel 600 light years to destroy or blow up our own homeland?" She pauses and watches the tabletop monitor, and from it she selects an image of a green landscape of rolling hills with occasional trees, grasses blowing in the wind. She pulls it up above the center of the table and lets it go, as each of the eight people watches it. "What we need, simply put," she lowers and deepens her voice, "is an Earth without *any* beings." Everyone intently listens while watching brown Irish Moiled cows grazing on the deep lush landscape near a farmette as white rabbits run past them. "Nothing living, breathing, swimming, flying, crawling, slithering—nothing, nothing should be alive before we land."

The members of Team 9 sit around the table awed at the images on the screen and in the hologram in front of them. They simply look at one another. No one says a word. Jacob, who seems like the youngest member of the Team, fidgets, tapping his fingers on the table. Elizabeth watches him and rolls her eyes. Maryam rises and walks to the window of the spaceship, lost in thought as she peers down at Earth. One by one, the rest of the Team join her. Huddling around the window, they forsake the monitor and gaze out, gaze directly, actually at Earth. Some seem lost, others entranced, and others even uncomfortable.

"That's enough!!" a thunderous voice orders. "That is not why we are here! We are not here to sightsee!" The voice roars.

"Scottie again!" whispers Jacob, putting his head in his hands. The members of the Team pull themselves away from the window, and quickly return to their seats at the table.

On the far side of the room, a pocket door in the wall slides open, and from it emerges a moving horizontal platform-like shelf. Atop the platform sits a small bony man, his limbs contorted and curled against each other. In spite of his size and stance, his grim mouth and fiercely-intelligent eyes are piercing and intense, and the Team members attend to his every word.

"You people are acting fools!" He declares in his distinct British accent. "I find it rather amusing how fast your intelligence dissipates the closer you get to Earth, your homeland. By now, I am hoping, you all would know the problem posed by Earth's beings," he says harshly. The people in the room watch him, listening intently, seemingly accustomed to his tirades.

"Perhaps I am being a bit unfair." He says with a touch of sarcasm. "Lest I forget, we were not all born with the same dispensations, shall

I say. However, as Keplerians, you all have had equal opportunity to improve upon your genetic baggage, the same one you had on Earth, have you not?" He says this with derision and the team remains silent, some shifting in their chairs, others contemplating their hands. "Ok! I don't mean it in a negative way, but let's face it, we are not at all all equal! We never were and never will be. Not even twins from the same womb, born within seconds, are equals." They continue to listen as they fidget.

"The problem with these miserable beings," he says pedantically as he points to the window, "the problem with this constantly moving, noisy, trouble-making, agitated, agitating bunch, is,... anyone?" He pauses and looks inquisitively around the room.

"Sex!" Maryam says emphatically.

"Thank you Maryam. Yes, sex, my dear friends" Scottie says. "And by sex I mean gender, sexual persuasion and..." he pauses. "the act of sex, sexual interaction with one another, it envelopes these beings into an unruly untidy doomed-to-fail package. It defines them, it consumes them, and as the result, it simply destroys them as worthy beings by reducing them to what they are: human beings."

CHAPTER 2: *SOULMATES?*

Morning sun climbs the Santa Monicas north of the flatland called lower Beverly Hills. Scarlet, a young woman in her thirties pulls on her stockings. Her long, sleek legs are perfectly shaved, her luscious lips are perfectly glossed and lined, and her body is supple and firm. She leans towards her vanity in the bathroom as she looks in the mirror to put finishing touches by her mascara. Her boyfriend Brandon stands at the doorway watching her. He comes up behind her, smiling at her in the mirror, and steals her gaze. She returns his smile and turns to kiss him, or rather to allow him to kiss her. Her long blond locks fall back and swing gently as she melts into his arms. Thousands of miles above her, in the Spaceship, a woman identical to Scarlet is lying in a glass incubator, with eyes closed and in a state of dormancy.

* * *

In Yorkshire, two bearded collies, one male and one female, bound across the sprawling lawn of a country estate. They spend every day in each other's company. Their dog walkers and masters are proud of them, and like their masters, they receive a treatment only fit for royals. Grooming, food, exercise, affection, what have you—they have it all. They have all they need, and more. They even have their own masseuse, which they think of as their personal belly rubber. Twice a day he comes over to assure the dogs of relaxed and tended muscles, sinew and bones. They are among the luckiest dogs on Earth, literally. And from their constant snuggling and mating, they seem to know this. They bound among the hedges and gardens, their masters clapping and calling to them. It seems as though they have been in love forever. Although they do different things on any given day, one thing is constant in their lives: Napping. They play and nap, eat and nap, and mate and nap, They then nap and mate, nap and eat and nap and play. Life is good.

In remote Patagonia, two proud roosters, Freddy and Shaq, in all their feathered finery, each surrounded by their brood of hens, live on neighboring farms. Over the fence that separates their territories, each cock crows without fail, at dawn. As they espy a glimpse of one another, they call and cluck their hens around them, then bellow across the fields to mark their space. Staring at each other like in an old Clint Eastwood movie, they will suddenly dash forward, ferocious and furious, in a charge. By the time they get to the fence, they are already airborne, slamming their bodies into the chain-link barrier and pecking at each other's faces and beaks. The hens behind them storm into a melee of screeches, flaps, and crows. After a five-minute brawl, though, bloodied and tired, the roosters retreat back to their homes, to their hens, their roosts, as they did the day before, and the day before that.

On the west coast of Africa, two bees dance in the air. The bees spin and chase each other through waves of flowers, landing on one petal and then flitting to the next, sipping each delicious nectar. Like girls dancing in saris, these worker bees flutter about, collecting nectar, while the male drone waits in hope of being fed, his life leaving little for envy, in a long line to mate with the queen.

Life is abuzz everywhere on Earth. On the monitor inside the spaceship, Team 9 devours all of it, a kaleidoscope of montage, teeming with life, flashing before their awestruck eyes. One monitor zooms in on New York City: Crowds swell down sidewalks, jostling, edging by, greeting, embracing, and bumping into each other. Everywhere in the world, people are walking, driving, flying, sleeping, some playing games, some running, and some even fighting. There is so much happening, everywhere. The Team members simply watch and marvel. They have never seen anything like this in their lives on Kepler-22. They've heard and read of it, life in all its flavor and color and form, but only in pictures, in books or in film. Now, here they are, watching it live on the monitors and from the window, the blue planet looming large as the Spaceship moves closer.

Scottie arrives from the door in the wall and joins the group. "That is how we all were. Each one of you, me, we were like that. We all lived, but not knowing why we were living, our main impetus and goal was to simply be alive and remain alive as long as possible! Now let us look at that man," he calls attention to one monitor. "See how he watches and salivates over that woman's breasts, a simple nutritional delivery system for infants. Look at this other couple quarrelling, as if at war, as if whatever minor matter is one of life and death. This tumultuousness of life here is largely a result of the attraction called sex. Even children succumb or aspire to it."

Jacob snickers at the sights on the screen.

"Please young Jacob," Scottie instructs, "have some sense. We were all more like these beings than you would care to know or acknowledge. In fact, some of us arrived at Kepler-22 with less intelligence and self-awareness than we see on some of these monitors. So please do not be quick to judge."

As the leader of Team 9, for the purposes of this mission, Scottie has been afforded considerable knowledge of each member's history and background. No one else in Team 9 possesses such knowledge.

"These earthlings believe it is romance, a human notion that gives impulse to action, a quest for love, a weird concept to be sure. Being attracted to each other is a physicality, the basis for which is attraction, a drive towards procreation, for promulgation of the race. This antiquated reflex has now become self-destructive, for their overpopulation is simply suicidal. See how some cheat and lie to each other simply because of the power of this attraction? Many a man has lost a political election, and even their lives because they have succumbed to this behavior. Each one of us was like that, one way or the other, some overtly, some covertly." Scottie says, almost lamentingly. He then sits down, as if fatigued from the thought of what he just said, and continues on with his tale.

"We died at different times," Scottie continues. "Some of us were children, and some were old when we died. But our deaths brought us to our current lives on Kepler-22, which has the same exact environment as Earth. About 170 billion human beings live on Kepler-22, a number equivalent to the number of all the people who have ever lived on Earth. Our planet is 36 times larger than Earth, sufficient, until now, to easily accommodate all. However, the rate of population growth on Earth will soon overpopulate and overrun Kepler-22 and thus, we need to re-occupy, in effect, to reclaim Earth as our own. This addresses not only the immediate problem of stopping the overpopulation but more importantly, of de-populating Earth."

A hush fell over the Team 9 members, having just heard the severity, the seriousness, of their mission. Each knew of their ultimate goal in travelling here, was to populate a new home. But now they realize that the complications and implications of doing so were clearly beyond their imagination or expectation.

"Scientists on Earth have just discovered our planet," Scottie continues, "and some are even referring to it as Earth's twin. Right in the middle of the habitable zone of the universe, the area known as the 'Goldilocks zone,' Kepler-22 exists in a band of space a certain distance from a star in which liquid water is possible." Scottie points to a hologram of Kepler-22 that has just appeared above the conference table. "As you can imagine, their attraction to our planet is not surprising. They don't know it yet, but it is in fact necessary for their survival."

"Our planet," says Maryam, looking longingly at an image of Kepler-22, "blue and tranquil, with clean fresh water, and a balmy 72 degrees, is perfect for us. Our planet is so big that because of its gravitational pull, we couldn't even get off the planet unless we used nuclear propulsion, which we did. We feel very safe there."

"Every animal on Earth has an exact identical twin on Kepler-22, born, for lack of a better word, at the same time," Scottie says. "While on Kepler-22, the twin remains in a dormant state, but ages and transforms, precisely as the body does on Earth, existing in a parallel world. The twin on Kepler-22 lies in a state of dormancy until its counterpart 'dies' on Earth. The twin remains dormant because it lacks what is known as 'spirit.' Only spirited beings have twin life forms on Kepler-22."

"Regardless of age or cause of death, a dying being's spirit immediately and instantaneously is infused into its twin on Kepler-22. The difference is that once the spirit is infused into the new body, which is identical to the old body, it makes the body eternal."

"Although the twin's body mimics the age of its human counterpart, it does not decay or suffer in any way from physical harm, defect, ailment, or illness. As you have noticed, there are no children on Keple-22. For those children who died on Earth, their twin has already grown to look like a 25-year old human being. This is so we can be sure their body is at its strongest and healthiest. Our system in effect rewards those children, for suffering an early death." Scottie says rather triumphantly as he paces back and forth.

Team 9 is rapt with attention, clearly being given new information. Andre's brow is creased and Maryam, as she is apt to do when she becomes contemplative, rubs her chin. Wang is looking up to the ceiling, as if trying to puzzle these details and anticipate the next point. Scottie stands in front of them, his arms crossed, watching and waiting for them to retain and ponder over this newly-found knowledge.

"Here, ladies and gentlemen, is where we differ from our counterparts on Earth. As the most perfect human beings, in fact, perhaps the most ideal beings in our universe, beset by no concerns of aging or death, we have no need to reproduce. By contrast," Scottie points to the blue planet framed by the window, almost disdainfully, "the humans and all the other animals and insects on Earth are far removed from this perfection."

Scottie sits back down, takes a deep breath, and continues.

"So you ask what we should do to rid Earth of these beings? There are countless ways to accomplish this, but I say, and I know you will all agree, that bestowing upon them in their current lives, the gift of freedom from physical selves, from their instinctual sex drive is most just and most poetic. It is of course, vital for us. There is only one effective way: We simply must de-sex them all!" he declares.

The group looks to each other and nods, while some raising their eyebrows.

*   *   *

"Can't we just watch them destroy themselves? After all, they are such savages with so many guns and bombs designed only to kill other human beings. Let them go at it? It's sort of entertaining, exciting" Jacob says. Wang giggles under her breath.

"No!" Scottie reacts. "I think it will be much more entertaining seeing how they behave once they are de-sexed, don't you? They may still be attracted to each other, but for entirely different reasons. For example, they may simply love each other, but not in the physical sense anymore. In any event, they will then die off, and yet, in a sense, we will not be killing them, at least not directly. They will still reap the reward of eternal life and health on Kepler-22."

"Riveting," says Jacob. "I still think it would be awesome to see them tear each other apart as they do with guns anyways. After all, like you said, they will come back to life anyway on Kepler-22."

"Jacob, my lad, you have had every benefit of the knowledge base available to you at home, and yet, still you come back to these kinds of remarks. If I didn't know better, I'd think you have retained some of your base human traits."

Jacob sneers, pushes back his chair, and laughs. "I'm a good actor though, aren't I Scottie? Aren't I?!"

Maryam, who is sitting next to Jacob, pats him on the back in a motherly way. "How do we de-sex them? She asks Scottie.

"We have the technology on board to de-sex the entire population on Earth. We will focus an unbroken stream of gamma-rays on the planet for only ten seconds, which will eliminate all living beings' reproductive genes. We shall watch for and notate the results," Scottie says in a professorial tone.

"This painless process," adds Scottie, "simply frees them of the need to mate or reproduce. Of course, to be sure, they will not feel a thing during this process."

Pranav, until now listening in sober silence, interrupts Scottie:

"You know that we were all born because our genes compelled it. Sexual desire and reproduction are gene-driven. How can we destroy the reproduction genes while still maintaining the genetic integrity of these people, including their emotional well being and balance, which if disrupted could interfere with our goal?"

"Ah, yes," answered Scottie. "You are perceptive and thorough. As you know, on Kepler-22, we do not reproduce and do not have any children. We have evolved beyond that. Here, once we de-sex them, all the ramifications of attraction will be eliminated as well. In other words, there will not be any gender, hence no need to worry about that type of attraction. They will become sort of like androgynous, where they can't tell if they are men or women, transgender, or any other gender for that matter. On Earth, all beings need to be attracted to each other, largely in order to reproduce. In animals, the attraction is baser, more primitive, but it is still the same concept, and it is real. They know what is needed, and they, rather dutifully, do whatever it takes to make it happen, the reproduction that is. Humans, on the other hand, need to be cajoled, extensively courted, wined and dined, if you will, until they become receptive to mating with a particular person. To humans, physical appearance and demeanor is considerably more important than it is to the rest of the animal species."

The members of the group look at each other, each seeming to consider Scottie's plan.

"Won't it take a long time for everyone on Earth to die, since we are planning for them to die natural deaths?" Wang asks. "Many people on Earth have lived to be 100-years-old, some even older. How long do we plan to be in this spaceship? Should we design some new hologram games while we are waiting?" She quips.

Scottie smiles and says, "It may seem like a long time to humans, but our time can speed or slow accordingly. After the ten-second gamma ray radiation, it will take us 10 days on the ship, that is all we need. At the end, every being on Earth will have reached its prime and died off. I guarantee it!" He says in a self-assured voice.

The members of the group look at each other again, and then with almost a melancholy expression they stare at Earth. Behind them, the dormant twin, named Scarlet2 lies diagonally in the glass incubator, her eyes closed, seeming quite at peace with the world.

CHAPTER 3: *THE LAST NIGHT*

On Earth, it is early Saturday evening in the Western hemisphere. People are engaged in what they usually do on their weekends. Some are out and about, laughing, eating, playing, courting, kissing, and even fighting. Some are at home and some are sleeping. Those who are together, including Scarlet and Brandon, the dogs, the roosters, and the bees are all intensely engaged in their own earthly trepidations. The cacophony of romantic gestures seems endless. Unaware, these Earth inhabitants engage in the dance of sexual attraction and love-making for which unbeknownst to them, will be their last time. Aboard the spaceship, the gamma ray beams are being prepared to be set in place. On the monitors are Team 9's selected specimen pairs: Scarlet and Brandon, the collies, the roosters and the bees.

Sitting on his platform, Scottie looks up from the monitors and says, "Tonight, history will be made for these Earthlings. This is the last night in which any new Earthling will ever ever be conceived."

As the earth gradually turns away from the sun on the western hemisphere, some of those living on the dark side start to go to sleep while some others make love. Scottie steps down from the platform and orders the two young men, Andre and Jacob, to prepare the equipment. Michelle, a skinny 25-year old with red hair and almond-shaped cocoa eyes, joins them.

The in-wall speakers on the spaceship play Shostakovich's Symphony No. 6, *The Execution of Stepan Razin* while Scottie takes aim. He pauses for a moment, looks at the members of Team 9. He then decisively pulls the lever, unleashing a cluster of light, a cloud of flickering multicolored light, hurling and expanding as it flies through space, racing towards Earth.

Team 9 watches the monitors. Where it is night, children are asleep in their homes. Where it is day, church bells toll. Minarets call the daily Allaho Akbar. Hindus pray. Muslims pray in Mecca. Jewish rituals are being observed in synagogues. A whirling dervish twirls feverishly. The luminous colorful cloud dims to a wide dark blue band as it enters the atmosphere. It then gently touches down on Earth, as if caressing its surface, embracing it. The band rapidly rings around the Earth, zigzagging and crisscrossing. The Dervish keeps twirling. In ten seconds, all of Earth is enveloped in a net of silky blue light.

In Beverly Hills, Scarlet and Brandon are deep in their romantic interplay. Strippers undress in clubs nearby. Hundreds of thousands of people around the world are sidling up to each other in bars, dance halls, and dinner parties.

In Yorkshire, the Collies are sleeping side by side. In Patagonia, the roosters are also deep in their slumber. On the west coast of Africa, the bees are pacing around inside their hive, protecting their queen.

A stripper slowly descends the pole as Donna Summer's "Last Dance" plays in the club. Her bare hips gently land on the stage as the blue ray cloaks every inch of the planet. Once she lands, she just sits there motionless. Her previously-raucous audience seems to have suddenly lost interest fall silent, and she herself seems dazed, lost. One of the customers, who is still clutching dollar bills in his hand, looks directly into her eyes and gently asks, "What is your name?"

"Candy," she answers.

"Come on, really, what is your real name?" he asks.

"It's Julie, from Allentown, Texas," she adds bashfully.

"Let's go grab a cup of coffee," he says as he gets up from his stool. Confused yet unusually relaxed, she gets up and walks off the stage. In seconds, she reemerges fully clothed and walks out with the man. The crowd around her begins to pocket their cash, as if they've forgotten why they had all these dollar bills.

The next morning, Scarlet gets out of the shower. Her long hair is wet and shimmering, and she is as beautiful as ever. She dries herself off and dons her robe. Her hair wrapped in a towel, she reaches for her lipstick, and leans toward the mirror to apply make up, as she has done every day since she was fourteen years old. She picks up the lipstick and brings it close to her lips. But she pauses, hesitates. She looks at it, befuddled, thinking of all the times when she has worn lots of make-up. She remembers the men who longed for her and wanted to be with her, and she remembers those who were intimate with her, without interest in wanting to get to know her. She wonders why she wasted all that time. She places the lipstick on top of her dresser in the bathroom, beside the mascara, blush, and eyeliner. She has no interest in any of it. Any more.

About ten minutes later, she emerges from the bathroom without any make-up on. She looks healthy and clean, and indeed radiant. Brandon is standing by the door, ready to leave the house. He says, "I'll be home around 7 tonight," and, as is his habit, leans over to kiss her, but instead he smiles, seemingly confused by his own intentions.

Scarlett just stands there staring at him with a serene half smile. He steps back, pauses, gives her a puzzled look, and walks out of the house. Scarlet looks at herself in the mirror on the back of her bedroom door. She intently peers into her own eyes, a querying look. She feels a lightness in her posture, some new kind of wonderment. She is suddenly very thirsty, and grabs a glass of water from the refrigerator. She then abruptly puts on her usual street clothes—mini skirt, high heels, and a Kate Spade handbag, and heads out.

She gets into her white BMW and drives down the picturesque hill beside their house. It is a beautiful sunny day in Los Angeles. Soon she encounters the usual morning traffic and slows down. On Route 101, she makes eye contact with someone in the next lane, a scruffy-looking driver with Mexican features. The man is wearing white overalls, and she could spy spots of paint all over it. They stare at each other for almost half a minute while the traffic is at a standstill. They both smile at each other. He then pulls up next to her and yells out, "Hello, how are joo?," in his thick Spanish accent.

She smiles and says, "Good morning."

"I love jour car. How do joo like it?" he asks.

"Oh, it's great. I just wish it had more leg room."

"Huh. And that's a provlem? Poor baby" He says sarcastically.

"Do you know, is it supposed to rain today?"

"I don't. But I know it's gonna be a hot one."

"I'm sorry. I gotta run."

"No provlem," he says, as he flashes a smile. "Take care. See joo!"

The traffic picks up again and they wave each other good bye.

Above, in the spaceship, the crew has been following this exchange on the hologram. Scottie points to the images. "You see, just yesterday she would not have talked to that man or even acknowledged him," he says. "That is because, on Earth, people generally, and often exclusively, became attracted to people with whom they have already interacted, or people who were socially acceptable to them. They also immediately judge each other based on their looks and engage in stereotypes on a regular basis. Besides, there has to be a reason to be attracted to someone they do not even know. For instance, the longer a time a person spends time in a room with a person of opposite gender, the higher are the chances of becoming physically intimate with that person. And also, the natural inclination to find someone within the same social strata as a means to physical intimacy has led humans to be wary of interacting with those they do not know, or who are not at their social or economic level."

"Most of the time they don't want to risk attracting or being attracted to strangers or new people due to fear of physical intimacy with those people. This hierarchy has stymied attraction or interaction with most strangers. People communicate at their own level of comfort, and are unlikely to interact beyond that. As you know on Kepler-22, everyone is willing, and in fact does interact with everyone else at any time, without any prerequisites or inhibitions. You can talk to anyone about any subject, even if you have never before seen or spoken with the other person. Their age, physical appearance, or social position is totally irrelevant to us on Kepler-22? right?"

The Team members nod their heads in agreement.

"On Kepler-22, unlike Earth, what matters is substance, not form. It is not who you know, it is who you would know by simply allowing it happen freely since everyone has a lot to offer."

The round table is now alit with monitors. One shows the Bearded

Collies walking and playing together. They begin to run after each other. Other dogs start to bark and enter the scene, but they lack the posturing dogs always display when they first meet. They don't sniff each other; they don't wait for one to show affection or submission. Instead, they happily simply play with each other.

Another monitor shows the African bees. "The bees' situation is unique," explains Scottie. "Generally, the actual mating process of bees happens above ground, in mid-air. After the mating, the male bee, which is called a drone, dies. The female bee lays the fertilized eggs later."

"Kind of sad for the male bee," comments Wang, with a half-smile.

"This is what humans would call a one-night stand," Andre says as he chuckles.

"A rather high price to pay!, I would say," Alex adds.

"Yes," adds Scottie. "But, now that we have completed the process of de-sexing Earth bees will no longer die due to this fact, because no more bees will mate. I think the drones will be quite thankful."

*　*　*

As Scarlet walks down the street, she realizes that no one else is wearing make-up either. Women, young and old, walk by her and some say hello, but not one of them is wearing make-up. Still they all seem prettily dressed and well-attired.

Scottie and the crew on the spaceship are watching her on their monitors as if they were peering through a window onto the street.

Elizabeth, watching Scarlet, says, "The way she walks, she seems liberated, at ease with herself and the world around her."

"Yes," agrees Pranav, "as though she no longer has to please anyone by her looks alone."

"She can be a woman, a person, plain and simple. She no longer needs to be attractive in that sense," observes Maryam.

"Remember, attraction is not necessarily a good thing," says Michelle. "It implies that only certain people can be attractive, at a heavy cost to the rest of the people. Remember, during our training, they showed us that movie called "*the Incredibles*"? You remember the kid with a funny awkward hair?"

"You mean 'Incrediboy'?" says Andre.

"Yes. He said, 'If we are all like Superman, then no one is.' In this case, by that logic, if all humans tried to be attractive, then no one really was."

"By contrast, in our world," Scottie breaks in, "there is no need to be physically attractive. Of course, that does not mean we promote ugliness or uncouthness. We simply do not equate being attractive with being beautiful. On Earth, being beautiful means pleasing people by your appearance and your presence. The result is that a majority of people are told to be like and act like a much smaller group of individuals deemed the 'Attractive' ones. The promise, the reward if you will, is higher social status, more wealth, longer life, and more physical intimacy."

"What qualities on Earth are considered attractive, and who gets to decide that?" Michelle asks.

"Yes, I'd like to know that too, and," interjects Andre, "by those standards, do we have any attractive people on Kepler-22?"

"The need to be attractive on Earth is based on the aspiration, the hope for physical intimacy," Elizabeth says. "The need can create social anxiety, the desire to be liked or the fear of being alone. Furthermore, the features deemed physically attractive can be used for enticement, even as a weapon, which in turn causes humans to lie and cheat, and even to kill. Some humans are consumed by their appearance, and by their need for sexuality. On our planet, sexuality is an anachronism, an outmoded, unevolved piece of evolution that has outgrown its usefulness. Two people are now capable of being very intimate with each other by sharing love, knowledge, and experience—more vital, more exciting, and more fulfilling experiences than sex itself."

Scottie, who has been intently watching the monitors, lifts his index finger and says: "On Earth, life can seem like a race towards what they call 'The End.' But life should be a race towards the beginning, the beginning of the eternal life, which is what we are blessed with on Kepler-22."

On Earth, Scarlet is walking out of a store. She is approached by a homeless man, who asks, "Hey, lady, can you spare a buck or two? I'm really hungry."

Scarlet has never been this close to a homeless person without feeling scared, repelled, or even repulsed. But this time she smiles, takes his hand in hers, and walks with him into a restaurant. It's lunchtime. She feels perfectly at ease doing this, she thinks to herself. They sit at a table and order a big lunch, while enjoying a pleasant conversation. She asks him whether he is married.

"Yes, I have four children," he says.

"Where are they now?" Scarlett asks.

"With their mother in the Projects," he says. "I miss them but I can't go back there. I just got out of prison and I can't find a job. No one will hire an ex-con. I can't add to their mother's burden by going there."

Scarlet promises him that she will drive him to see his kids the following week.

All this time, because of Scarlet's generously low-cut blouse, the homeless man has had the opportunity to peer down into her cleavage, but he does not. He is simply interested in his lunch and in his conversation with her. They then order a healthy dessert. Across the room in the restaurant, a wrinkly bald old man is sitting with a young man, chatting. At another table, an older, heavy-set woman is enjoying a drink with a young man. In fact, as it turns out, in this restaurant, like in others, today, people are sitting with whom they really wanted to sit with regardless of class, gender, age, or even stature. They all seem at ease and at peace with each other. Only a day earlier, at the same restaurant, a fight had broken out when two homosexual patrons were attacked by five men who had walked in off the street. The homosexuals were badly injured and taken to the hospital, and the police were called to apprehend their attackers. The staff is still a bit shaken.

Pranav, on the spaceship, watches. "They are already acting as if looks and even gender do not matter." He observes.

"It also explains why we all look exactly the same as we did when we were humans living on Earth," observes Elizabeth. "Because, by our standards, we are all beautiful on Kepler-22, no matter how we look. More importantly, we are all healthy."

Pranav gleefully agrees. He knows that if a man is 90 years old when he dies on Earth, he comes back to life on Kepler-22 as an entirely healthy 90-year-old person, free from all diseases. But he looks exactly the same—he is a healthy elderly person. On the other hand, if the person dies at an age younger than 25 years old, that child will wake up on Kepler-22 as an eternal 25-year old. Nevertheless, the bodies of everyone, whether they are 30- or 90-years old, have the same physical capacity as a healthy 25-year-old.

CHAPTER 4: *THE ENCOUNTER*

"Now we are ready for our first experiment!" says Scottie in an excited almost boyish tone. "We need to ascertain to see whether our people can survive on Earth, given its often unforgiving and harsh conditions. On Kepler-22, we've tested in laboratories, our resistance to diseases, our tolerance of the climate, and tried to anticipate all varieties of dangers. We now need to know if the Earth is ready for us before we send billions of people down here. Would any of you like to volunteer to be sent down there to assure that our survival simulations are truly correct?"

On the monitors, the crew watches scenes of scorching sun, howling winds, blizzards, hurricanes, sandstorms, earthquakes, and tsunamis, combined with scenes of brutal wars and diseases.

Michelle says, "Don't look at me! I'm not going. I like the calm constant 72-degree days on Kepler-22."

"Me too," adds Wang. "It's too uncomfortable, too primitive down there."

"Not my cup of tea either," says Andre, as he walks away from the monitors.

"We've paid our dues already—we shouldn't have to go through it again," Alex complains.

"I was kidding!!" Scottie yells. "None of you are going down there. We have already prepared for this experiment. Right, Elizabeth?"

"Right you are!," Elizabeth exclaims. "During our preparation, we assumed that none of us would be willing to go and live on Earth even for a short period, at least not under the current circumstances. I don't blame you. It is dangerous. So, we decided to do something that we have never done before outside of the laboratory: we can activate a person's dormant twin, someone who is not yet dead on Earth and send her down there. And so, we have brought along a twin for this purpose." He points at Scarlet 2, lying in a glass room nearby.

"Sending a twin down would be too risky," objects Pranav.

"I agree," says Maryam. "Having two living versions of the same person is an untenable situation, given the fact that every active body needs to have a spirit, a soul. We have only one spirit for this individual but two bodies. I don't see how it is possible. Besides, activating a dormant body early flies in the face of our whole theory of population control, which is why we are here in the first place."

"There is a solution," says Scottie in an unusually deep and contemplative voice. He gets up and opens the door to the side room,

31

where Scarlet's lookalike, her twin, is lying in a glass incubator. He leans on the glass box and sighs as he looks up, as if he had been hoping to find something there but hadn't found it. Then he looks up to the ceiling and starts pacing the floor. "Under some certain conditions, there is a ten-day window within which we can activate this twin and have her share the spirit of her human counterpart. At the end of the ten days, if we absolutely must, we will simply eliminate the primitive Earth's version. The condition is that both the Twin and her Earth counterpart always have to be in close proximity of each other. They must never be apart, even for a millisecond." Scottie lowers his head as he concludes. "I think we can learn a great amount about the human spirit, from the interactions we will observe between them."

Scottie turns again to look at the woman in the glass box, Scarlet 2. Then he taps on the box with the palms of both of his hands, as if playing a drum. "Let's send her down!" he orders as he abruptly walks away from glass box.

Alex stands up and moves to a panel in the room next to where Scarlet 2 is. He puts on goggles and lowers a translucent shield between the two rooms. He touches the screen and from the top shield of the incubator, a red ray beams towards the eyelids of Scarlet 2.

The team stands rapt at attention in a semicircle around the door. The awakening of a twin is a serious and solemn occasion for

Keplerians, and not one that anyone has ever witnessed, Alex thinks to himself as he directs the red ray at Scarlet's closed eyes.

Scarlet 2's upper cheek twitches, and Maryam gasps. Elizabeth leans in to see more clearly. Scarlet 2's eyes slowly open, and then blink repeatedly. Every team member seems to hold their breath. Scarlet 2 looks straight up to the ceiling of the Spaceship, breathing heavily, her chest heaping, rising and falling with each new breath. Alex is immersed in his work, pushing buttons, his expression invisible behind the goggles.

The glass box pivots upright and locks in place. It looks like a mummy's coffin. The lid to the box slides aside without a sound. Scarlet 2, now staring straight ahead, sees everyone. Virtually expressionless, she steps out and walks past them toward the star-shaped pedestal in the middle of the spaceship. A violet ray hovers over her head and envelops her body. Team 9 had seen such a beam before, when they partook in their training for their long travel to Earth. They know, through the ray, she is being prepared for her journey to Earth. That is indeed how they were able to travel 600 light years in a short time.

She is being readied to accompany her counterpart, Scarlet on Earth. Will she be well-equipped for the encounter? Alex wonders as he works the machines. The team gathers around her, the light ray brightens, dims, and changes colors. As the seconds tick on, the colors increasingly lighten to white, and soon her image is obscured by a strong white light whose particles shimmer and move, so bright that the team has to look away. Suddenly the light caves in on itself, and Scarlet 2 is gone. She has been transported to Earth.

*   *   *

The last few days have been quite busy and hectic for Scarlet. For days on end, she has felt this strange urge that she needs to help people, and because of that, has not spent much time at home. From desolate shelters to heart-breaking hospitals, and even to busy divorce courts, she has travelled, to support those impacted by misfortune. She feels as if she owes it to everyone to help in whatever way she can. In fact, she has become obsessed with wanting to help people, hoping to change their lives for the better. But she is beginning to realize that she is still human, and she needs to eat and get enough sleep. She trudges on.

The afternoon's steady drizzle changes to rain. Despite the rain pouring down on her windshield, and the fog from the inside, Scarlet can still make out the faces of dozens of women drivers. None of them are wearing any make-up. She smiles at them, and becomes happy when they occasionally return waves and nods.

Five minutes before reaching her house in lower Beverley Hills, Scarlet remembers that she needed to get something from the store. She pulls up into a strip mall, but there is no place to park. She drives on and tries to find parking on the street. The first spot she finds is almost two full blocks away from the store. She parks, and realizing that she does not have an umbrella, she dashes through the rain. Suddenly, the image of her mother, who died five years ago from breast cancer, comes to her mind. This is not unusual for Scarlet. Ever since her mother's death, Scarlet has had almost daily flashbacks of her, of her illness and her death. She remembers brushing her mother's thinning hair in front of the mirror one rainy afternoon.

"Mom, you always wanted me to be perfect," she said.

"I did and I do. You had a tough childhood, so I want the best for you, even more so now." Her mom looked at her in the mirror. "You can only try so much, but never give up trying. Your dad left us when you were a kid, and now he has re-entered your life. He was wrong to do what he did, but whether you give him a chance is up to you," she said. "Even when I am gone, I want you to remember to be the way you are, which is the way I always wanted you to be. You are perfect."

"Mom, you might lose your gorgeous hair now, but it will regrow," she said, stroking her mother's hair.

"I hope so, my love. I really do."

As her mom's memory replays in her head, Scarlet continues to run through the rain, which is now torrential, making her completely soaked, dripping with rainwater. She reaches a building and tucks herself into an indent in the wall to wait for the weather to subside. She looks at the glass door next to her and notices a person on the other side. She does not pay attention but she feels the person is looking at her, staring at her. Feeling a bit uncomfortable, nonetheless she quickly glances at the person. "She looks like me," Scarlet thinks to herself. On second look, she realizes that in fact, the person is her mirror image, even wearing the same clothing. She assumes that it is her reflection she sees. But she moves and the reflection doesn't follow. She points and the reflection doesn't. She becomes confused, uncomfortable, and scared. She does not know what is happening.

"Is this a joke, a prank?" she asks aloud facing the other person. Beginning to tremble in her drenched clothes, she glares at the image, the person behind the glass door. As she does, Scarlet 2 opens the door, steps out and stands next to her. Scarlet's eyes bulge. She tries to move, to run, but she feels as if she is paralyzed. Her limbs are numb. She wants to scream, but she can't. She feels as if she is simply frozen in place.

Suddenly, Scarlet becomes frantic and regains her strength. Wet and terrified, she dashes out into the rain.

Scarlet 2 runs next to her, side by side. Scarlet runs harder, and faster but cannot gain on her. Nonetheless, she keeps on running, panting. Scarlet 2 running at the same pace calmly says to her: "You don't need to be scared of me! I am you, and you are me! I am here to help you!"

Scarlet starts shrieking as she continues to run. "I don't need any help! Who are you? Leave me alone!"

Scarlet 2 stops. Scarlet continues to run. Then she looks back at the woman, her own image, herself, standing in the rain. The woman looks lost, and Scarlet begins to feel towards her as she did towards the others she's helped the last few days. She stops, turns around, and calmly walks back while the rain pounds the pavement.

Still terrified, Scarlet asks, "Who are you?"

Scarlet 2 does not utter a word as the raindrops slide down her face. Scarlet 2 does not look real somehow, as if her image is hollow, yet moving. And then Scarlet 2 whispers, "Tell me about Mom."

"My mom?!" Scarlet's heart drops as she asks, again visibly shaking with fear and confusion. She then steps back, as if defiant. The rain begins to turn into a soft drizzle.

"Yes, Mom."

Scarlet cannot understand why this stranger who looks like her is asking about her mom. She's now more puzzled than terrified. The drizzle lightens to a trickle, and Scarlet feels herself breathe normally, feeling a sense of calm, a serenity that she has never felt before.

"She was great," Scarlet sighs. She cannot believe that she is even having this conversation with a total stranger but she continues. Somehow she feels at ease with this person. "As a matter of fact, she was my soulmate, the best friend, anyone could have. But she had a tough life. She single-handedly raised me and my sister by working full time and she never let us feel that she was suffering. She was great. That's all that I can say. She was simply, truly great." She is crying by the time she finishes her sentence. She sees that the woman who looks like her is weeping too. Suddenly Scarlet feels as if she is no longer scared of this person, her mirror image, but she remains suspicious.

"Why do you want to know about *my* mom? Do you work for the government? Why do you look so much like me?"

Scarlet 2 smiles and says, "It's a long story. Let me just say that I am you and you are me. That may not mean like much to you now, but it is the truth."

"Are you trying to drive me crazy because I am an activist? Is this a CIA plan?" she asks, irritated again. "If so, you can go back to them and tell them they cannot beat me in this fight. There are too many people out there like me, and if they want to fight, well..."

Scarlet 2 touches Scarlet's lips with her finger in an assuring way. "*Shhhh.* You have nothing to worry about. I was not sent by anyone from your planet."

"You are an alien? I might believe anything else but that!" Scarlet snickers as she looks around, hoping someone else heard the woman. "I'm sorry. You seem like a nice person but you are wasting your time and mine." Scarlet turns to cross the street, and Scarlet 2 follows her.

"I live on a planet called Kepler-22, and I have the same exact features as you do. That's because I am you after you die. When you were born on Earth, I was born on Kepler-22 at the very same moment. In fact, I came to be the second that you were conceived. I'm sure you don't believe me, but it's true. Basically, we live on two separate planets, but we are the same person, in every way that you can imagine."

"So, you are telling me that you're a walking, talking dead person? I know, I believe in heaven and hell. But I don't believe people who are dead can walk around and talk to the living like you're talking to me. I don't know what you're up to, but it seems mean," Scarlet says somewhat calmly.

"I think that's strange too, but I didn't make the rules," Scarlet 2 says. "I guess you could call Kepler-22 a kind of heaven." She stares into Scarlet's eyes.

Scarlet, who was terrified just a few moments earlier, finds herself drawn to Scarlet 2. They seem absorbed in each other. The pair walks back to Scarlet's car side by side, and Scarlet seems deeply engaged in conversation with Scarlet 2 as they get into the car and drive home. She even forgot to buy what she had gone to get from the store.

Brandon is not home yet, and Scarlet 2 looks around the apartment as she talks with Scarlet. She walks over and looks at the photographs on the kitchen counter. She asks Scarlet, "Is that Mom?"

Scarlet is taken aback. "Yes, that's her. That's *my* mom. But if you are me, shouldn't you know her?"

"I do know her," Scarlet 2 says rather as-a-matter-of-factly. "I know she is on Kepler-22. If she saw me, I know that she would be particularly nice to me because she is so close to me." She says as she weeps.

Scarlet runs to Scarlet 2, not listening to what she just said. "How is she? Is she as beautiful as she was on Earth?" she asks.

"I'm sure even more beautiful than in this picture. We have no diseases on our planet. Everyone is well preserved. She looks like this, but more lively, more vibrant. She was so very kind when she was on Earth. Now, she is even kinder, more giving on Kepler-22," Scarlet 2 says, sitting down on a stool at the kitchen counter.

"I can't tell you how much this means to me," Scarlet says as she hugs her twin and cries on her shoulder. "You've given me the greatest gift."

Outside, dusk fades to night, and the street lights flick on and car lights bustle down streets in this urban oasis. Scarlet wipes her eyes, and starts dinner.

A while later, a car pulls in the driveway. Brandon runs in. "I'm so glad you're home. I know it's only been a few days since we've been home this early, but I missed you so much," he says, as he hugs her.

"You've been crying, though. What's the matter?" he asks.

"So many unusual and unbelievable things," Scarlet says. "I'd like you to meet," Scarlet turns around to Scarlet 2:" I'm sorry. Do we have the same name too?" She asks Scarlet 2.

"He can't see me, only you can," Scarlet 2 says to her.

"Who are you talking to?" Brandon asks.

"Just myself," Scarlet says, giggling. "But enough about me. How was your day?"

"Different," Brandon shakes his head in wonderment. "It was very different. I don't know, but no one seemed themselves. People seemed strange, but strange in a nice way. They were unusually nice to each other."

"I noticed the same thing. It must be something in the air. I just feel more free somehow, lighter, happier. I forgot to tell you. The other day, a homeless guy asked me for money, so I brought him to lunch. We talked about so much. I don't know why I was afraid of homeless people before. So many people in need," she said.

Brandon interrupted her. "That's so weird, because today, this lady at the office came up to me and asked me whether I could give her my opinion on her marriage. Imagine that! She wanted me, someone she has never spoken to for more than two minutes in the last ten years, to give her advice."

"I don't know. I don't understand it. But whatever it is, it feels good," she says, looking out the window, staring into space.

Brandon plunks himself onto the couch and switches on the television as Scarlet 2 looks on.

"At the Vatican today, a large group of nuns stepped out and mingled with the general public, even dancing with some men!" the TV announcer says, in a surprised tone. "There is niceness kindness in the air everywhere. No one in the world knows what is happening. Similarly, Muslim women in many parts of the world have shed their traditional hijabs and are demanding that the law be abolished." His co-anchor continues, "And all over the world, traditional Jewish women are removing their head coverings too. We have a live report from our correspondent in the Middle East. Amelia?"

"I am standing here in main square of the city of Riyadh, Saudi Arabia. In my 20 years covering this area of the world, I have never seen or heard anything like this. People are coming out of their houses, gathering in large groups. They do not seem to be protesting anything. They are simply acting very differently. They mingle with each other as they never did before. Everyone is in a friendly festive mood."

A Muslim woman is interviewed. She smiles and has a curious sparkle in her eyes as she talks. "We don't need to cover our hair anymore." The woman is covered from head to toe with thick black cloth, as the woman unwraps her head scarf. Happy, smiling children circle and dance around the camera, waving peace signs, playfully shoving one another. There is loud cheering in the background as security guards stand watch, looking puzzled but relaxed. "No one seems to have any interest in the way we look any more. We are treated with respect and dignity, no longer simply objects of desire.

Our husbands love us for who we are, not for what we look like. They don't look at other women. This is so liberating!" she declares as she saunters away from the camera into the crowd.

"In California," the newsman continues, "men and women have taken to the streets in support of equality based on something other than looks or gender or race. It sure seems reminiscent of the civil rights movement of the 1960s, except this time, it is not about gender or color, it is about us as human beings. Everyone seems to suddenly treat everyone else equally in all aspects of the society, in private and public, not just by the government."

The newscast returns to the anchorwoman. "In San Francisco, many clubs are admitting everyone without regard for their appearance or gender, as long as they appear clean. The City Council is considering a measure tabling reforms for equal rights based on the sudden lack of need for them. In other news, retailers have reported that condom sales have sharply dropped."

Scarlet smiles as she watches. She too feels liberated, content. For her, there seems to be no more need for heavy makeup, high heels, and fancy Gucci handbags. No more pressure to conform, she thinks to herself. "The world is changing," she says. "I don't know what changed but I feel good about myself, so much so that I can talk to others without any inhibitions or reservation. I feel as if I don't have to risk having men think I'm coming on to them if I talk to them, and

I feel like they won't come on to me. I feel so safe! Brandon, do you feel different too?"

"I'm cool with whatever's happening," he says as he switches off the TV. "I don't mind either way. But you're right. I don't feel much of a rush to do things or get anywhere, other than to just be. In fact, I just feel like turning in. I'm pretty tired." He goes into the bedroom. Scarlet follows him after she flicks off the lights in the living room.

In the bedroom, Scarlet rummages through her drawers, pushing away teddies and slinky negligees to find her extra large t-shirt at the bottom. For a moment, she wonders why she even owns such impractical sleepwear. When she gets into bed, Brandon curls up to her.

"You know I love you. Don't you Scarlet?" he says as he kisses Scarlet on the cheek.

"I do Brandon. I love you too." Scarlet 2 sits in the corner, looking on, innocuous and quiet.

Over the next few days, Scarlet 2 shadows Scarlet's every move. And, after three days, Scarlet doesn't even seem to notice her presence. Rather than thinking about her twin, Scarlet has been preoccupied with memories of her mother.

In her mother's last few weeks, when she'd lost all her hair from the treatments, and had become so frail and weak, she said to Scarlet

"If I could do one last thing in this life, it would be to see *Cats* in New York with my favorite person in the world—you!"

Scarlet had called her mother's doctors and asked them if travel was unsafe in any way. They assured her that making her mother happy was the best medicine. So Scarlet made all the arrangements to travel to New York. They walked around in the City. They window shopped on Fifth Avenue. They rode in a horse-drawn carriage in Central Park. One afternoon they went to the Guggenheim Museum. When Scarlet surprised her mother with the *Cats' tickets*, her mother cried of joy, and said "And I thought life couldn't get any better than this. I love you more than anything, my dear sweet girl."

Scarlet tears up just thinking about those words, and all over again, she feels like a five-year old little girl, always tagging along, wanting more and more from her mother. Wanting to run, to tag along after her, to never let her out of her sight. But when her mother died, so young, Scarlet had to let go, and she knew it. Life just isn't fair!, she thinks. Maybe she's thinking this way, because now Scarlet 2 is at her side, and it's Scarlet's time to take care, to protect and to understand how Scarlet 2 must feel.

Scarlet takes Scarlet 2's hand, and rushes to her car. They get in and Scarlet drives fast, too fast, to the Westwood Cemetery where her mother is buried. Holding Scarlet 2's hand in hers, she rushes to her mother's grave. They find it beneath a pine tree, and Scarlet caresses the headstone, kneels down and kisses it.

Scarlet 2 looks on. She kneels down beside Scarlet, and they both somberly stare at the tombstone. Scarlet begins to cry. She looks up, whispering, "I want to talk to Mom." Her voice, trembles and her lips are quivering. "Can you help me? Is there a way to talk to Mom?"

She then turns around, slowly gets up, looks at Scarlet 2 and says, "Where is she now? I want to know where she is. Is there a heaven or a hell? Is she living, or is she dead forever? Please answer me. You must know. Tell me!" Scarlet cries as she clutches Scarlet 2's hands.

Scarlet 2 stares at her for what seems to be an eternity, but she remains silent. Finally she takes both of Scarlet's hands, folds them between her palms, and presses them. "Your mom is with all of us, on Kepler-22 Scarlet," she says somberly.

Team 9 is attentively watching the scene between Scarlet and Scarlet 2. Scottie says, "Before we decided to bring Scarlet 2 with us, we checked out her whole family, even remote ancestors." He grins. "Her mother is a very happy, content and kind woman." Scottie suddenly sounds somber. "She will never suffer again. She looks the same as she did before she was ill. When she arrived, she looked ill, but her good health has helped her look rejuvenated again. She does not remember Scarlet, as none of us remember our Earth families. You see, our memories are no longer important as tools to guide us. But she does sense her daughter's love, and she does return love to her. You see, memory is a very tangible entity in comparison to love. We are capable of loving somebody or something without any memory associated with it. Memory on Earth is a vehicle, a means to an end. But on Kepler-22, we have no need of it in any other way than to remember and exercise emotions. Our emotions are alive and well; we just know how to channel them now. Without memories, positive or negative, we have no need for hatred, or other emotions such as jealousy, which are built upon negative memories."

"With that in mind, please understand that there are people on Kepler-22," Scottie continues, "who have done terrible things on Earth. They have killed, raped, destroyed, pillaged, lied, and cheated while they were on Earth. What they did wrong on Earth is not remembered. But whatever good we have done is retained, as a reflex of sorts. We even have people who have committed the most heinous of crimes, like Hitler, Tamer Lane, Pol Pot. We do not believe in sin, nor in punishment, because we have eradicated a need for both. We are not primitive like the people on Earth. We have everyone on Kepler-22. We have people who have done wonderful things on Earth as well. We have Siddartha, Mother Theresa, Einstein, Martin Luther King, and countless other leaders who have done amazing things for the Earth people. We all live together, as one, understanding the fundamental truths of existence. Earth life to us is the means to our end, the means to an existence that is infinite and timeless, an existence that is nourishing and devoid of pain and suffering."

"Scarlet may not understand this, but once she dies and comes to Kepler-22, she will have no need to understand, because her memories of Earth will be gone. The discomfort of missing loved ones, that sense of loss, will be absent once she joins her fellow Keplerians," Scottie says.

Andre shifts in his chair and says, "But when somebody has suffered on Earth, shouldn't they remember what happened?"

Scottie responds, "As I was saying, there are billions of people up there who were wronged when they were on Earth. People have been subjected to oppression from the very start of our genus. Even at the time of the cavemen, people became the victims of one another. They were beaten, abused, raped, and killed. They suffered tremendous injustices. Many witnessed their loved ones being tortured while they themselves were subjected to abuse. There were perpetrators and there were victims. Now, and forever, these people exist in serenity and peace, on Kepler-22."

"On Kepler-22," Scottie proudly continues, "there is justice for all. There is no preference for one type of person over others. No one is superior to anyone else. No one has any possessions or needs to have any possessions, so there is no conflict over material goods. And there is no love of the possessive kind that you people have on Earth. We love without any restriction. We love everyone because there is no other way to live."

CHAPTER 5: *THE DEPARTURE*

Under the bright California sun, Scarlet slowly twirls on a grassy hill behind her house. Scarlet 2 watches and mimics her. Together they spin, their arms aloft, their faces lifted to the sun, smiling as the grass fronds brush their skirts, as they swoosh by. They run and laugh as the soft breeze sweeps the grasses in waves. It is February, but on this hill near Los Angeles, it feels like springtime.

That night, Scarlet has a nice quiet dinner with Brandon. She still has not mentioned Scarlet 2. From their 24th story window, the couple looks out on the city as it bustles with life.

After dinner, Scarlet leaves her home to attend a meeting of a group called Occupy LA. The group advocates economic freedom and justice for all. When she enters she is surprised to see among the people seated around a circle, many of whom are her upper-middle-class friends. She finds that when she tells people about her work with the group, they are without exception, supportive, and she is even further surprised to hear one very wealthy friend agree with the tenets of the group.

Scarlet's father, who lives across the Valley, is a U.S. Congressman. He seems so proud of Scarlet's decision to enter "politics" and excited to help her get started. Although he is not at the meeting, but Scarlet fills him in after she has left the group. Within days, he receives an invitation from an old college friend, now a Washington D.C. socialite, to attend a national meeting concerning social injustice. He cannot attend, he tells her, But he asks Scarlet whether she might go in his stead. The next day, Scarlet flies to D.C., and with her father's friend's friends by her side, she meets with several congressmen and women, who express interest in her cause. While she is there, she meets a number of other socially minded people, and becomes energized with a desire to help groups who help free prisoners, visit hospitals, and meet with sick children and their parents. In a short period since the De-sexing Ray hit Earth, she has become a completely transformed woman. She no longer feels as if the world revolves around her and her needs. Scarlet 2, as always, is by her side.

When her plane touches down in LAX, Scarlet is exhausted from the sleepless night but happy. She picks up her BMW at the long-term parking lot and begins to drive as if she is not tired at all. It is 5 o'clock in the morning on a gray drizzling day. The road is wet and slick, and she weaves in and out of traffic. Scarlet 2 sits in the passenger seat and does not know how to suggest to Scarlet to pull over. Scarlet knows she has a lot to do after this important meeting. She wants to get home as soon as possible, so she presses on the gas pedal.

Her cell phone beeps and alerts her to a text message. She reaches into her bag on the seat beside her, and lifts the phone to read, "We did it! People are getting their houses back from the banks! YOU DID IT!!"

Scarlet is so gratified and thrilled by this news that she gets teary-eyed. She excitedly texts back, "We are all one! *WE* did it!"

But as she types, the car skids on the wet road, and begins to hydroplane. She loses control, veering in and out of the highway lanes, but in seconds, she hits the median strip. With a loud bang, her car becomes airborne. Scarlet cries out, and Scarlet 2 looks on, helpless to make any change. Scarlet frantically tries to regain control but her vehicle lands on the other side of the median strip and faces oncoming traffic. A tow truck flying along at high speed rams into her car, smashing the driver side. Her car flips and becomes airborne again. Scarlet's head hits the roof of her car at high velocity, instantly breaking her neck. She immediately loses consciousness. Her head dangles on the headrest of her seat.

Scarlet 2 continues to watch from the passenger seat, shaken by what she has just witnessed and seemingly without understanding. As the traffic comes to a standstill, Scarlet 2 simply sits there. Drivers from other cars run to assist Scarlet, but Scarlet 2 is invisible to them. She looks at Scarlet's mangled body, covered with blood, and then she gets out of the car. She turns around and stares at Scarlet's bloody face for one more moment. She smiles and walks down the side of the highway, ignoring the police cars as they close off the road.

Scottie and the crew are watching the screen from the spaceship. Team 9, especially the young ones, are visibly shaken, the ability to empathize being alive and well on Kepler-22 is not lost on the Team. Scottie asks Andre and Michelle to pick up Scarlet 2 from the highway, and they immediately transport her to the spaceship. Without uttering a word, she returns to her incubator and she closes her eyes for a few seconds as everyone looks on.

She reopens her eyes, looks around, and tries to stand up.

Alex yells, "We have to send her up now! Now!"

Scottie leaps forward and motions to Scarlet to stay still. He looks at her and smiles. Then he says, "Welcome to our world, my dear. Welcome!" He then motions up with his hands while pressing a button.

Scarlet's body simply vanishes, as if she has never been there, and she opens her eyes as if she had just awoken from a long-night's rest. She is sitting on a plush grassy hill. She feels a great sensation of restfulness, peacefulness, and a bit of weightlessness. She has nothing on her mind, nothing at all. There is no memory of anything, past or present. Nor is there any anxiety about the future. She feels that she simply exists at peace with herself, and the world around her. Somehow or other she feels elevated and liberated. She is freed of all humanly chains, restrictions, and inhibitions.

On Kepler-22, Scarlet's mother is the first person to greet Scarlet. The crew on the spaceship continues to watch her on the monitors. "That is always the tradition: one's loved ones await you when you get there," states Scottie.

Scarlet's mother holds out her hand. Scarlet looks puzzled for a split second and hesitates, and then a sense of calmness and serenity pervades her again. She visibly relaxes. She extends her hand and holds both of her mother's hands as if they have always been the best of friends. Although they do not acknowledge each other as mother and daughter, they can both feel a deep and utter bond of love between them.

They hold hands and walk together into Harsin City, the capital city of Kepler-22. Scarlet's mother shows her around. Scarlet does not remember what happened on Earth, or even that she is from Earth, but she feels as if a cloud has been lifted, and she has become far more coherent and insightful. She has now tapped into the collective reservoir of knowledge and wisdom.

She surveys her surroundings. It is a beautiful spring day on Kepler-22. As the soft breeze caresses her face, she continues to stroll with her mother. The birds are singing, and she sees a field full of dogs, sheep, Neanderthals, people, and lions. Roosters stand side by side on fence posts. Many in the fields are sitting in circles on the grass, deep in discussion; some are lying down, enjoying the gorgeous day; and many are playfully running after each other. The difference in species is not noteworthy to her.

Scarlet passes by Benjamin Franklin, who is engaged in conversation with Carl Sagan and Euclid. Mohammad, the Islamic prophet, is having a friendly argument with Jesus and Moses while the Pharaohs look on. Scarlet sees a group of 25-year olds running around. "I will race you to the fountain," one of the young men says. The others have already started to dash even before he finishes his sentence. People from 25 to 100 years old, are playing running games. There is a reassuringly confident sense of eternity in the air.

Scarlet and her mother pass some women, all dressed in their own era's garbs. They smile at Scarlet and her mother as they walk by.

John Lennon walks up and says to Scarlet, "I am always waiting, you know."

"How wonderful!" Scarlet responds.

CHAPTER 6: *OF THE BIRDS AND THE BEES*

Freddy, the rooster, strikes a pose, his neck erect and straight, his feathers ruffled and flexed, sure to attract the glints of sunlight that will bring out his most iridescent greens, blues, and purples, Freddy, a proud rooster rules his brood, each morning displaying how vigorously he will protect his hens and his domain.

Across the fence, less dazzling perhaps, with feathers speckled black on white, Shaq, the other rooster rules his turf. His morning crow, considerably less strident than his neighbor's, does not seem to hinder him in his role as protector of his brood. Instead of running and hiding from his crow as Freddy's do his, Shaq's hens emerge from the henhouse to watch him sing his morning song.

However gentle or not with their broods, the two roosters never miss the next duty of their day—a full-on run towards the chain link fence, which separates them. Dashing towards their nemeses, leaving their hens in the yard, day after day after day, returning, some days more bruised and bloodied than others, the pair adheres to this seemingly pointless exercise with instinctual duty and much aplomb.

During the morning battle, the hens simply sit and watch, seemingly content with the mayhem. Once the fight is over, the hens welcome each rooster upon his return.

Watching on monitors far above, Pranav explains, "You see, the hens actually select the successful male, not just because of his fighting abilities, but also because of his appearance. Hens prefer a dominant appearance, and the display of this dominance over other roosters always helps even more."

The night the De-sexing Ray hits the Earth, Freddy and Shaq mate with their hens and then lie down to sleep. When dawn arrives, they first crow, and then, by force of habit, strut around their hens. After one final overview of their domain, they step outside, Eying each other in the distance. They assume their attack posture and careen towards each other. But as they bear their talons, and make a dash, they suddenly slow, and become aware of the grass beneath their feet, the sun on their backs, the worms and bugs and other sweet morsels hiding in the soil. Near the fence, Freddy stops to examine a worm in the dirt, and Shaq walks towards him, swinging his lowered head from side to side through the fence to see if he can make out what Freddy has found. Soon the pair are walking side by side, each stopping while the other grazes or pecks at. These two arrogant roosters, Freddy and Shaq, the old arch enemies, sated and full, now sit down to rest in the tall grass, warming themselves in the sun. No more war.

The bees are similarly affected by the De-sexing Ray.

"Before the ray hit, the bees, of a completely different genus, were attracted not just to each other but to the flowers from which they feed," says Wang.

"The flowers also seem to be attracted to the bees," says Michelle.

"Yes," agrees Wang, "there is a symbiosis between bees and flowers that is rare between species, particularly with one being an animal and the other a plant. Flowers, with their brightly- colored petals and fragrant scents, attract their pollinators. Some attract only certain types of pollinators, like hummingbirds. Bees, because of their body hair, can collect pollen, which benefits the flowers by enabling them to reproduce."

"The benefit to humans is incredible," says Pranav. "Humans eat the honey that bees make from nectar. They have a particular taste for something called 'chocolate,' the result of pollinated cocoa."

"Alas, we had to destroy this symbiotic relationship," observes Scottie.

"Does that mean that flowers no longer emit fragrances and their colors are no longer bright?" asks Michelle.

"No, not at all. You know how beautiful Kepler-22 is, with flowers and the wonderful fragrance in the air," says Scottie. "The De-sexing Ray has simply stopped the bees from pollinating. The flowers now will pollinate through the breeze and no longer through the bees."

"Even before De-sexing, the bees were dying in record numbers anyway," observes Alex. "They are disappearing in huge numbers from their colonies in the U.S. especially, but also in Europe. This is part of what the humans called Colony Collapse Disorder (CCD). Interestingly, the bees always die away from the hive. One day they would fly away and never return," says Wang. "Some human scientists said that if the bees disappeared and there was no more pollination, humans would have only a few years to live."

"But we don't have to worry about that anymore, now do we?!" observes Scottie.

CHAPTER 7: *A DE-SEXED WORLD*

Andre is keeping an eye on the monitors. "It seems that the dogs are waltzing around, the bees are still buzzing, the roosters are in harmony, and the people are still doing what they used to do, but more peacefully. Is this it?"

"Not quite!" exclaims a slightly-annoyed Scottie. "Their life has been permanently turned upside down. Look more closely this time!"

In the Middle East, two Muslim women are walking down the street, still wearing their burkas. As a stranger passes by, he stops and talks to them. One of the women drops her veil to listen to him. He is asking for directions, and the woman with her veil in her hand, points to where he should go. Still confused by where he is trying to go, the other woman grabs his hands and walks with him for a bit to show him.

"This was unheard of just yesterday," says Scottie. "Yesterday, both that man and those women would have been severely punished. In fact, that woman would not have talked to the man even if there was no threat of punishment. The man would not have even looked

59

the women in the eyes. But now they are forming a purely innocent relationship devoid of ulterior motives."

In San Francisco, at a well-known gay bar particularly famous for its Saturday nights, a bouncer stands in front of the door, admitting people. He is talking with his friend, telling him how his own partner is simply "going cold" on him. "I am not really sure how; I can't put my finger on it. But it's almost as if he is no longer interested in me in the way that he used to be. The attraction is gone. Maybe I am getting to be an old man."

"There must be a bug going around. I have no interest either," says the friend. They both laugh rather apprehensively.

On a crowded Bangkok street in the red-light district, people flock to food shops while the prostitutes in the windows look around, eating their lunch. Many are chatting with their supposed patrons. Some men buy food for the women and join them in conversation. The women are still dressed in their colorful lingerie, but many are donning sweaters and robes. They seem to be more in need of comfort than customers.

In California, Hugh Heffner, the founder of Playboy magazine is watching his girls swim in his pool at the Playboy mansion. Three of his favorite companions, one of whom he has married, are in the water. The young women are tossing a blue ball to each other, and laugh as they toss. He smiles, watching them from the side of the pool, as he sips on his Martini. The women's hair shimmers in the California sunlight.

When they take time out from playing, he yells out to one of them: "You're a fish! Where did you get your love for water?"

"My dad used to have this huge boat," the girl answers. The others turn to listen. "He would take my sister and I out on the water any chance he had. That was when he was home, which was every other month or so. We would do synchronized dives off the gunwales and then race around the boat. I'll never forget those days."

She climbs out of the pool and grabs a towel to dry off her bare breasts. She seems a bit nostalgic. The other girls follow her, putting their hands on her shoulders.

"I wish I had a dad like that," one of them says.

"You were lucky," says the other.

"No, I'm the lucky one here," Hugh says. "Where is your father now?"

"He passed away years ago."

"I'm sorry sweetie," he says.

"Thanks Hugh," she says.

About 20 minutes later, the girls emerge in sweatshirts and running pants. They pull up chaise lounges, surrounding Hugh. Just a week earlier, at about this time, they would all engage Hugh in a sex party with him as the lead man. But now for hours, they sip drinks and dine, talking about their favorite childhood memories until the night gets chilly and they move inside. Hugh participates in their talks, but nothing else.

In New York, Lady Gaga prepares for a video in her dressing room, with her latest boyfriend in tow. She steps out in a pair of transparent overalls. In her vast loft, her video crew is playing volleyball. They stop and start filming her. The video is so unlike her previous ones, however. There is nothing in the video about sex or sexuality. It is about people, not about men or women. The video becomes an instant hit.

The divorce courts of the world are filled as usual. But many couples are seen sitting together discussing their children, rather than fighting with each other. The lawyers linger in the hallways, shaking their heads, and wondering whether to wait out this new-found détente to end or to give up and look for a different line of work. The couples with mediators are brainstorming about how to make better lives for themselves and for their children. No one is whispering or hiding. All private information is divulged and shared. The idea of infidelity is moot. The maneuvers of self-interest are absent. The adults act as adults, and work together to decide what is best for their soon-to-be former spouses, and for their children.

At a wedding, a bride and groom dance knowing, albeit intrinsically, that they will be best friends, not husband and wife. The bridesmaids, holding hands with the best men, dance and encircle the newlyweds. Weddings are quickly becoming a rare scene.

Jewish orthodox women remove their wigs and head scarves, embracing their male friends, holding hands with them and even dancing with them.

On the spaceship, Elizabeth watches the monitor with tears in her eyes. She says, "Love should not be the privilege of the few as it is on Earth. It should be universal like how we love on Kepler 22."

"Why are you crying?" Michelle asks.

"I just get emotional when I talk about love. To me love is innate. It is a feeling unreserved, something for everyone and everything. Do you know what I mean?"

"I'm not sure," admits Michelle.

"Well, I guess I mean people are experiencing that you can love the person sitting next to you on the bus as much as you love your child, as much as you can love someone across the globe, someone you've never met and never will."

In Midtown Manhattan, office secretaries sit at their desks without any make-up. At a Catholic bishops' convention in Rome, it is announced that male priests will be able to marry "if they choose to do so." In American high schools, young athletes date the nerdiest, homeliest girls in their classes, while cheerleaders ask the geeks to rub suntan lotion on their backs. Planned Parenthood announces that due to a lack of patients, it is closing its doors forever. Maternity wards suffer the same fate. Victoria's Secret goes out of business, while book sales skyrocket. More and more people sit around chatting with each other. A commercial on TV shows a middle-aged plain-looking woman, her face free of make-up, saying, "Don't hate me because I'm beautiful!" Billboards display women and men interacting with each other in gestures of kindness, suddenly a profitable message. In Malibu beach, a seniors' shuttle rolls along the boulevard blasting a song. Inside the passengers sing, "I am sexy, and I know it..." X-rated movies, magazines, and books have become collector's items.

And everywhere, people attend more and more funerals, and animals mourn their lost members. No one is being born.

CHAPTER 8: *SEX: A NECESSARY EVIL?*

As the crew on the spaceship watches in awe, Michelle wonders, "I understand that there was a biological aspect to sex, but even so, why were humans so obsessed by it?"

"It is a dilemma, indeed," says Maryam. "If sex were simply biological, why were they more consumed by it than by any other biological activity? Even those who were castrated remained subjected to it. They seemed to be more obsessed by it than all the other animals on Earth. In fact, there is even a right-to-sex movement attracting many followers."

Jacob asks bashfully, "By the way, I am curious. If our goal is to stop procreation, and these people are so obsessed by sex, why did we not simply sterilize the male population, so the whole world could continue to enjoy sex if that is really what they wanted?"

"That wouldn't have worked," Pranav answers. "Firstly, some species do not need the male to impregnate the eggs. Also, if we had simply eliminated the male sperm, then human beings, being as industrious as they are, would find another way to fertilize the eggs.

In fact, they had already begun doing that. The de-sexing process, in contrast, does not discriminate. It affects everyone and every being regardless of gender." The group begins to gather around the table, sitting down as they become more intrigued.

"You see," says Scottie, "until now, humans on Earth were completely, and in my opinion unreasonably, tied to sex and sexual relationships—even those who did not engage in it. Young and old were led to behave in ways which would satisfy their sex drive, even subconsciously. Their books, movies, and even religions were often directly or indirectly tied to sex. Some called it 'intimacy,' but the result was always more physical than emotional."

"When this phenomenon called puberty hit us, suddenly testosterone and estrogen began to interact, leading to a wild and fuzzy feeling, which humans call "love.' Some people called these feelings 'lust,' which seems to rule during puberty and for many the rest of their lives."

"Does that mean that they needed lust before love?" asks Jacob.

"Not necessarily," Maryam says, surprising Scottie. "While the initial feelings may or may not have come from lust, what happened next—if the relationship progressed—was attraction. When attraction or romantic passion came into play, people often lost their ability to think rationally—at least when it came to the objects of their attraction. The old saying on Earth 'love is blind' was figuratively accurate. Often oblivious to any flaws their partners might have, they idolized their objects of affection and could not get them off their minds. This overwhelming preoccupation and drive was indeed part of their biology."

"In this stage, the stage of attraction," Pranav says, picking up Maryam's train of thought, "they as couples would spend many hours getting to know one another. If the attraction remained strong and was felt by both parties, then they usually entered another stage: attachment."

"But we know that not all of this attraction was simply because of their behavior," says Pranav."

"I know a thing or two about love." volunteers Elizabeth almost seductively, as she looks away.

Andre interrupts her. "I know about this! I know about this! I have read about it! Are you talking about that almost empty feeling they experienced, when their palms sweated, they turned red, and their hearts beat a hundred times a minute?"

Pranav politely interrupts Andre. "This was due to the chemicals that the humans' brains were releasing. The first one is Dopamine, which was the culprit behind the feeling of pleasure, humans feel during sex. The second chemical was Norepinephrine, which increased your heart rate and made you feel anxious or excited. When combined, these two chemicals led to the feeling of love, which was illustrated by a highly-animated activity, and the sense that you could not take your mind off of that other person."

Alex says, "Let me add that men developed this feeling of "love" or "lust," depending on who you ask, this chemical reaction, a lot quicker than women. After all, men, being a more visual species, processed these chemicals faster, even after one meeting of their female counterpart."

"But all this talk about sex is only window-dressing, mind you," Scottie chimes in. "Biology did nothing but propel genes towards a future. To do this, it had to lay the groundwork by building a solid mechanism to maintain gene propulsion. For instance, another chemical in the brain, 'oxytocin' had various functions in the body, such as inducing labor contractions and milk ejection, but from the perspective of evolutionary biology, its main function was to bond humans to their children for life. It also served to bond them to their mates, at least long enough for each person to fall in love with the child so that it will have two caregivers for its long childhood and adolescence."[1]

"That sounds so cynical!" says Wang.

"But it's true my dear! I am not making it up! This is what Marnia Robinson, a former corporate attorney, and now a clear authority on sexual relationships on this planet, and many others have found," responds Scottie. "Dopamine is the neurochemical, which was the one that 'motivated humans to go after the reward'. Dopamine governed the feelings of wanting and yearning, yet the experience of liking or enjoying something was probably due to opioids. Opioids were the human 'brain's own morphine and endorphins.' Dopamine drove them to eating and to have orgasms, but the pleasure of the actual orgasm or of eating chocolate arose from opioids goosing the reward circuit. In essence, dopamine was never satisfied."[2]

Pranav adds, "Marnia Robinson also says that 'these neurochemicals work hand in hand together, always supporting each other. For instance, after a frenzy of copulation, a male rat will lose interest in a female," Pranav continues. "But—and this is interesting—should a new female show up, he'll perk up for long enough to service her. This is because oxytocin rises in rats for hours after mating, and that in turn leads to riskier than normal behavior."[3]

"Those rats, always taking risks!" chuckles Andre.

"This is Earth science, Andre," Michelle whispers in a motherly voice.

"This process can be continued until he practically dies of exhaustion," Pranav continues. "It is what the Earth scientists call the Coolidge Effect. The Coolidge Effect is linked to humans' post-orgasm hangovers. The reason the rat loses interest in his first partner is that he's getting a weaker and weaker dopamine surge from her. No dopamine surge, no interest!" He walks around the table. "She is not perceived as 'rewarding.' The same thing happens with humans. The thrill is gone, and Partner No. 1 becomes uninteresting."[4]

"But remember, 'humans were still primed for anything that would jack up their dopamine again!" Scottie chimes in.[5]

"Yes," says Pranav. "In fact, as Robinson says, "oxytocin and dopamine were the yin and yang of bonding and love. Dopamine furnished the kick, and oxytocin made a particular mate appealing, in part by triggering feelings of comfort. You needed both chemicals, acting on the reward circuitry at ideal levels, to stay in love. If you blocked either oxytocin or dopamine, mothers would have ignored their babies."[6]

"The good news for people on Earth was that making love while avoiding sexual satiation was the loophole in biology's plan for our love lives," Elizabeth adds. "Aren't I right Scottie? This was the secret that the ancient sacred-sexuality sages stumbled upon: making love with lots of affection, without the dopamine-driven highs and lows of conventional sex, seemed to keep neurochemical levels balanced."[7]

"You are so right, Elizabeth," says Pranav. "We also know that 'the more oxytocin humans produced, the more receptive to it key nerve cells became.' This is the opposite of dopamine. In addicts, dopamine receptors start to decrease as the nerve cells protect themselves from overstimulation. Addicts then needed more and more of their chosen drug—in effect, more and more dopamine. Luckily for people on Earth, they didn't need an ever-increasing 'fix' of oxytocin to maintain the sparkle in their romance. Daily bonding behaviors could make one's partner look better and better—at least in one's own eyes. This was why daily acts of affection, with fewer orgasms, could strengthen the bonds between sexual partners."[8]

Pranav says, "Oxytocin was associated with significant benefits, both emotionally and physically. In fact, oxytocin may be the answer to the question: What was the mechanism by which love and affection positively affected the humans' health?'"

"That is what they called Sex!" Scottie declares.

"Can you sum up what sex did for humans?" asks Andre impatiently.

Pranav patiently smiles and says, "Sex stimulated the release of certain hormones, including testosterone for men and estradiol or other estrogen for women. The release of hormones primarily regulated the sexual drives of an individual."[9]

"You see, we humans, had made our own bed and had to lie in it: which came first? the biological physiological aspect of sex or the psychological metaphysical?" asks Scottie. "It was a self-fulfilling philosophy, sort of like the chicken and the egg. Humans like to create their own fantasy worlds and then proceed to live in them. But then when things do not turn out the way they want, they get flustered and think that something has gone wrong on their end, and then they decide to change it, not always for the better though."

"In fact, in many ways, our world on Earth was an illusion, a creation, a concoction by us. We labeled and named everything and then attached an emotion to it. For example, we first named anything, which scared us as 'bad' or 'monster.' We then decided to call other things with the same name, every time we had the same feeling of fear. We created the number 13, and then we said it was bad luck. Similarly, we created the concept of male and female and the word sex and tried to fit it all into our incomplete explanations in order to justify their validity. It is a ruse, a trick that we historically played on ourselves. We were victims of our own minds, our own actions. After all, on Earth, we were always suckers for a good trick, especially the ones, which we had invented ourselves."

Scottie continues, "In fact, sex is a clever ploy by genes to lengthen their own lives. That right-to-sex movement that you talked about Maryam was indeed concocted and manufactured by these gene rascals. If we stop sex, as we now have done, we will manage to for the first time outsmart the genes and nip them in the bud once and for all. And that is precisely what we intended to do."

CHAPTER 9: *A CHILD IS REBORN (JACOB)*

"I don't remember anything about my childhood, yet I know that I too was born on Earth," says Jacob. "All I know is that by Earth's standards, I am twenty-five years old and will be forever."

"You were indeed a child, a mere nine-year old, when you died of leukemia. Your parents loved you, and you loved them," Maryam says.

Maryam points to images on the monitors of a little boy running around on dry leaves with his grandfather. As Jacob examines the image, it starts to become more crisp, and like a slow film reel, slowly turns animated. The autumn leaves crackle beneath their feet as Jacob and his grandfather walk together. The red, yellow, and orange leaves color the ground like an Persian carpet.

Jacob's grandfather snaps a picture with his camera as Jacob runs into the leaves, spraying them up like water at the beach. "Jacob, be careful not to slip," his grandfather cautions.

Jacob seems to forget the leaves and runs towards the house. He grabs a basketball from the side of the driveway and throws it towards a hoop over the garage doors.

His parents look on from inside the house. His mother yells, "Jacob, come inside, we need to have lunch soon. You know we are going to the doctor."

"Okay, Mom, just a second," he calls. He throws the ball several times trying to make the basket.

Inside the house, the family seems distraught and concerned. They are huddled around the kitchen counter, talking. Jacob's dad says, "I think we should see another doctor. This is ridiculous."

"David, we have seen four specialists so far, and they all say the same thing: it is leukemia. Why can't you accept it?" Jacob's mom says. "You can't keep hoping, David. You simply can't," she whispers. David lowers his head and covers his face.

Jacob's uncle, a roundish middle-aged man with a goatee looks at the parents and says, "This is reality. I cannot imagine how difficult it is for you, but you can't neglect the other children and your lives, especially when there's nothing you can do but enjoy the time you have left together. Your lives, everyone's lives, are being devastated by this."

Jacob finally gets the basket, as his grandfather cheers him on. Jacob runs in the back door, throwing his skinny arms in the air mimicking to aim with a basketball. "Mom, I got one! I got one!"

His grandfather gingerly steps in the back door.

"That's wonderful honey," she says to Jacob.

Jacob looks around at the grown-ups surrounding the counter. "Mom, why is everyone whispering?"

"Come, eat something. You must be starving," she says.

He sits down and smiles as he eats. He looks at everyone with his bright blue eyes and devours his sandwich. Everyone seems stoic. An hour later, he and his parents leave the driveway and head towards the hospital.

"I don't think it is going to be an easy year for the Yankees," the doctor says as he feels under Jacob's jaws for swollen glands.

Jacob is on the hospital bed. He smiles and says, "Not as long as we have Jeter! We'll beat LA with Jeter! He's the greatest!"

The doctor smiles. "The nurse will be in soon with some food, and dessert!"

He walks out of the room with the chart in his hand. where Jacob's parents await him. "He will likely have some pain in the next couple of weeks or so. The pain will gradually increase, so he will need strong pain relievers. He will also have to go through extensive chemotherapy, and I am prescribing Cytarabine."

Jacob's dad asks, "Will he last through the World Series? He lives for it."

The doctor pauses, looks David directly in the eyes, piercing through his pupils. "Anything is possible. But I don't want to give you false hopes." He walks away with watery eyes.

Jacob's parents hold each other and weep quietly. They brush the tears from their eyes before they enter his room.

Jacob sees their faces, and he seems to sense the seriousness of his situation. He sits up and looks his parents straight in their eyes. "Mom and Dad, I have one thing that I want you to know. I am not dying. No! I am not dying. I am just going to a different world, a different place, a more fun place. You are coming too, Mom! Come visit me, Mom! Will you?"

Jacob's mother hugs and kisses him all over his face. "Of course, I will my darling."

"Eew, cooties! Mom. I love you, but this is embarrassing!"

"I'm sorry dear," she says smiling. "You always know just what to say, don't you my little man?" And then she turns around and walks out into the hall, where she crumbles onto a bench and quietly sobs.

With his father by his side, Little Jacob closes his eyes and falls asleep.

Within three weeks, his condition dramatically worsens. As doctors and nurses administer more and more medication, his body becomes more and more resistant to the medicine. One afternoon, little Jacob looks up at his parents and his brothers and sister and in a half-dazed state, simply shakes his head. He peacefully closes his eyes.

He awakes refreshed as a young man of twenty-five, perched on a grassy meadow. The soft breeze blows through his auburn wavy hair.

He gets up and smiles at the people standing by him. They all greet him, and a friendly old man takes his hand and shows him around. He has arrived on Kepler-22.

Jacob looks up from the monitor, with tears in his eyes. "That was me, wasn't it?"

"Yes, it was Jacob," Scottie answers.

"Who was that old man who greeted me? Was he related to me?"

"Yes," says Scottie. "Your greeters are always the ones who loved you the most on Earth. In this case, it was your other grandfather, who died five years before you did."

Jacob then sees himself starting to interact and socialize with others on Kepler-22. For a moment, he looks up at the new sky and stares at the many moons hovering above.

The monitor shows images of Jacob's funeral. The funeral home is packed with people. There are many children from his school, his friends, the girl he had a crush on, his teachers—even the kid who beat him up when he was in the first grade. They are all at the funeral, and they are all weeping.

"They must have loved me very much," he said. "But I don't remember them. Are my parents still alive?"

"Don't worry. They will be with us soon," says Scottie. "You will not recognize them, as no one on Kepler-22 recognizes anyone from their previous lives on Earth. All you will remember is kindness—a cozy, warm feeling that you had on Earth. That has not changed. We only show you this memory bank, because you are part of our team, and we hope it will help you understand that our mission may seem to cause pain on Earth, but you know well how temporal that pain is, in light of where these people are headed if we don't do something."

The monitor shows Jacob's parents, only two years older than they were when he died. They are still mourning their son's death.

Michelle looks on as Jacob watches his parents. She says, "I'm 25, so I must have been a child too. Can I also see what my family was like?"

CHAPTER 10: *MICHELLE'S FAMILY*

On the monitor, a narrator with a crisp voice tells Michelle's story as everyone watches:

On an unusually warm afternoon in late May, 1984, Michelle and her sister are playing on the front lawn while their mother is busy packing for their vacation. They live in a suburb of Boston. Michelle's father, an engineer and part-time associate college professor is not home yet. He is still in his classroom at the Community College. The two girls, Stephanie, a bubbly four-year old, and Michelle, a two-year-old play hide-and-seek under the shades of the trees. Their mother, Natalie, is a young shy woman from Thailand. Natalie is anxiously packing because the whole family is going away to visit her husband's parents in Dayton, Ohio. Everyone is excited about the trip. The girls are now on the front lawn singing as they hop on the pink magnolia petals, which cover the grass under the tree.

Natalie calls to the kids, "Come inside girls; have some snacks."

The girls giggle and run inside. Natalie makes them their

favorite—peanut butter and strawberry jelly on English muffins. As they eat, Natalie sings for them.

<u>Hush, little baby don't you say a word.</u>

<u>Papa's gonna buy you a mockingbird</u>

<u>And if that mockingbird won't sing,</u>

<u>Papa's gonna buy you a diamond ring</u>

<u>And if that diamond ring turns brass,</u>

<u>Papa's gonna buy you a looking glass</u>

<u>And if that looking glass gets broke,</u>

<u>Papa's gonna buy you a billy goat</u>

<u>And if that billy goat won't pull,</u>

<u>Papa's gonna buy you a cart and bull</u>

<u>And if that cart and bull fall down,</u>

<u>You'll still be the sweetest little baby in town</u>

When the girls finish their snack, Natalie puts them in their room for a little nap. She cleans up the kitchen, and shuffles through the clutter by the back door to ready for the trip. She begins setting the suitcases and bags on the driveway, to put in the car once her husband comes home. It is getting very dark and she is worried. She does not like to travel at night.

Michelle's father has just finished giving the final exams for his students, and they say their farewells before their summer break.

"Goodbye Professor!" they shout as they leave the classroom.

"Goodbye everyone!" he shouts back.

He starts to drive home in the family's bright yellow 1980 Ford Pinto Station Wagon.

The kids are up and about after their naps, running in circles having been sprung from the confines of their room to hear again that they are going on vacation. They watch for the lights of their father's car, the awkward-looking wagon, and as soon as they spot him rounding the corner and heading towards the house, the girls cannot contain themselves. They cannot wait to get in. They have gone on trips in this wagon before and they always loved it. They run outside and dance as he pulls into the driveway. Natalie is standing at the door, smiling and watching the kids. Michelle's father jumps out and kisses Natalie and his girls.

"Come on kids. We are going on a trip!"

The girls yelled: "Hurray!" and began to dance around the car. He glances at them, and looks at his wife approvingly. She kisses him.

"We should get going; it's getting late," she says. She runs inside and quickly changes into what she always called her traveling dress, a white airy dress with tiny pink rose buds printed all over it. Michelle's father puts on his night-driving glasses, as he calls them. By the time they get on the road, it is about ten o'clock. Her dad had been working at the College since seven in the morning on that day. He feels sleepy but wants to drive all the way so as not to waste a whole night. The kids are excited. He is excited. His wife is excited. Both Michelle and her sister Stephanie are strapped to their child seats in the back of the two-door car. Her mother has her seatbelt fastened, but her father does not buckle up.

Michelle and Stephanie sing, "Row row row your boat, gently down the stream!" to the sound of their mother's clapping. An hour into the drive, Stephanie unbuckles her seat without being noticed.

"Dad," she says. "How long before we get to Nana's house?"

"We just left baby! It will be a while." He knows it is going to be a 14-hour drive and they are only now on the Mass. Pike. The car is hot, and the car air conditioner blows only hot air. He pulls down the windows half way, making it hard to hear.

Natalie takes out a book to read to the kids. Michelle's father keeps driving, his eyelids feeling heavy already. But he keeps pushing, willing himself to keep them open. He thinks maybe exercising his eyes would be a good idea, and it seems to work.

But when he turns onto Route 15, a parkway in Connecticut, he closes his eyes for a second, but he quickly catches himself. The car veers off a little, but he manages to straighten the wheels. No one seems to notice. The girls are busy in the back, reading and playing. He keeps on driving. From time to time, he glances at Natalie, who is reading *Winnie the Pooh* to the kids. She looks radiant, he thinks. He looks in the rearview and sees Michelle, her eyes filled with joy, the kind of joy, he thinks, one sees in a child when he or she is content, simply happy, with no worries in the world whatsoever. He then takes his eyes off of the family and looks at the road. This is one dark road, he thinks. He wishes there were more traffic, more cars, more lights, so he could stay alert. But it is close to midnight. The Parkway is quiet and all he can hear is the sound of the wind and Natalie's faint voice, reading.

He lightly pushes the gas pedal, hoping that the speed will wake him up. He then tries to fiddle with the radio. There is nothing but static. There are no stations within range. "Damn it!" He murmurs. He keeps on driving. He can hear Natalie's voice, but it is now sounding more like a murmur in a dream, a real dream. He can hear Michele's tender sweet voice, asking her mom: "Where does Winnie actually live? In the forest or in the trees or in the trees in the forest?" He can then hear her laugh because she has made a joke. He closes his eyes. The Wagon veers to the right, hits a large tree on the side of the road head-on, and at the loud sound of the impact, he opens his eyes and slams on the brakes. The Wagon flips over. The windows shatter, and both he and Stephanie are thrust out of the car. He has lost his consciousness. Stephanie lands next to the road and remains conscious. With the car overturned, gasoline begins flowing down from the windows. Four-year old Stephanie watches, as the car becomes engulfed in flames. Both Michelle and her mother are burned beyond recognition. Stephanie and her dad are both badly injured, and when the ambulance arrives they have to be airlifted to the hospital. One of Stephanie's arms is so badly mangled that it has to be amputated that same night. Both she and her dad stay in casts for months.

On the spaceship, Michelle sobs as she sees what happened to her family. She now remembers that when she arrived on Kepler-22 as a twenty-five-year old, she was greeted by a beautiful young Asian woman. "So she is my mother, isn't she?" Michelle says.

"Yes," says Maryam. "She is the one who loved you most on Earth, and that was why she greeted you as you arrived on Kepler-22. Do you want to see your father and sister on Earth?" Maryam asks.

"Yes!" answers Michelle. "I would."

She looks at the monitor and sees Madison Avenue in New York City. In a tall glass building, a young woman gets off of an elevator along with two others. She is dressed in a grey suit and walks fast. Michelle notices that although she is carrying a briefcase, one of the woman's arms is not in plain view. Then she realizes that the woman's right arm is artificial.

Taking sympathy on Michelle, Maryam arranges for her to be briefly transported to outside of the elevator, on her sister's path. Michelle smiles at Stephanie and follows her. Stephanie smiles back, looking somewhat puzzled she pauses, and then walks away. She looks good, Michelle thinks to herself.

Michelle then finds herself in a long corridor in front of an office, with lots of books on the shelves. Her father is working behind the desk in the office. He is now a tenured university professor. She sees her own picture as a two-year old, along with pictures of her sister and mother on the desk. He looks grey and crouched.

"Hello," says Michelle.

"Oh, hello. What can I help you with?" her father asks.

"Oh, nothing, nothing." Michelle beams at him.

Looking somewhat puzzled, he asks, "Are you a new student at Brown?"

"No. I—I—just wanted to know how you are doing."

He smiles and says, "Well, thank you for asking. I'm fine. Should I know you?"

"As long as you are well," says Michelle. "That is what counts for me. We are all well too. Have a good day!" She turns around and quickly rushes out as he stands there with a half-smile, looking pleasantly puzzled, watching as she walks rapidly down the hall and disappears from view.

CHAPTER 11: *AN ENGLISHMAN IN OUR MIDST*

"How did *you* die Scottie?" asks Andre, rather bluntly, yet curiously. Scottie pauses and lowers his head. He seems somewhat perplexed as if he did not expect this question. Although as the chief of the Mission, he is equipped with the knowledge of every member's origins, including his own, he seems uncomfortable sharing his own story. Feeling the weight of everyone's eyes on him, he ultimately capitulates. He lowers his head and begins to speak, but this time in a thicker-than-usual British accent:

My name is Scott James Fitzgerald. When Hitler began attacking and bombing London on September 7, 1940, what historians called the London Blitz, I was an eighteen-year old lad. I was the only child of a bureaucrat father and a nurse mother. My mother, Betsy, was a truly selfless caregiver. She would go out of her way to please my father and me, almost to a fault. My father was a tall man, and his mustache had begun to gray ever since I knew him. He was the quiet, classic nerd. His strict daily regimen consisted of getting up at five in the morning, reading the *Times*, and then catching the bus at seven to go to his job as the assistant City comptroller for the City of London.

Although my mother was a devout Protestant, I was raised in a non-religious household. My father never practiced any religion, and my mother only made me go to church with her on major holidays. Although I was baptized and taken to church to kneel at the altar to receive the elements, bread and wine, but that was about the extent of my so-called religious activity. In fact, my father dissuaded my mother from bringing me to church on a regular basis.

By 1940, England was officially at war. In a span of just a few months, almost one million British homes were destroyed by German bombing. Because I was the only child, I became exempt from military service. However, I was still required to do non-military work, and soon became employed by the war industry. From early on, I loved physics. In fact, I was quite of fond of science in general. I constantly explored and conducted my own experiments, even as a young lad.

I began to work in a lab at the university, experimenting on the new ways to develop weapons. Although the work was quite tedious and the conditions were harsh, I enjoyed my work. I worked long hours, seven days a week. I loved to work, but I must admit, I loved to argue about the meaning of life even more. That's probably why I read philosophy any chance I got.

When the war was finally over, there was an immense amount

of new information available on the subjects of my interest. This was like heaven. I simply devoured it. I was always a voracious reader, but I was far from being what they term a geek like my father was. When I was 23 years old, I finished my university degree; but I wanted to become a scientist, so I needed further study. I applied to Oxford and was admitted in the field of astrophysics, a life-long dream for me. So, I studied very hard. I ultimately became a professor at Oxford while I lived at home. My father died when I was 30 years old. Afterwards, my mother aged quickly, became very frail and began to develop symptoms of amnesia. Sometimes she would not even recognize me, her only child. When I was 35 years old, she died. I was lonely and soon married. We had two children, a boy and a girl. We lived a relatively quiet life.

Outside of the house, I was a very energetic, loud, and animated professor. My students seemed to love it when I would run up and down the steps in my large classrooms, raising my voice, and asking questions from my students. There was never a dull moment in my class.

After my last class of the semester in May of 1985, I had left campus when I began to feel dizzy. I went home and asked my wife to call my doctor. He told me to go to an emergency room. I did, and once there, I was tested. They found a large lump on my head, which later was found to be a cancerous tumor. Within two months, I was operated on. I died on the operating table due to a blood clot.

Scottie's eyes well up with tears. He looks away and continues. "At the time of my death, I really wanted to see my son's graduation from college but I never got to see it. My wife died many years later and is up on Kepler-22. But we don't recognize each other even though I greeted her when she arrived. That memory is simply not there in my mind at all. Both my children are still alive on Earth. Now I am here to bring the rest of my family home. And I will," He says, wistfully looking at the ceiling. Team 9 sits there quietly, listening. Andre, however, seems unimpressed. He had expected much more from the leader of his team. After all, Scottie was the most colorful member of the Team, with a vast and eclectic knowledge of things and concepts. He had wanted Scottie's death to be much more dramatic, such as dying heroically while fighting the Germans on the ground, a mad scientist exploding his lab, or as a fighter pilot crashing into the Atlantic Ocean after having sunk at least a few German U-Boats.

Elizabeth gets up from the table, and walks over to Scottie, putting her hand on Scottie's shoulder.

Scottie gently pats Elizabeth's hand, looks up to the crew and smiles. "Everyone of us has a story on Earth, and for each of us, although we don't remember the details of our stories, we have the capacity to empathize with ourselves as if outside of ourselves. Remember that we are all one, all bound by the same origins in humanity. No one story is greater than the others. Our lack of memory upon arriving on

Kepler-22 enables us to empathize with each other as equals, to learn to love and exist on a truly unbiased plane, and for this, we must be grateful. As we each learn our stories, we will treasure them. But I urge you to remember to cherish the other's as much as your own. This is the gift of being a true Keplerian. The purpose of our informed knowledge in this mission assures our tenderness with the subjects of our mission."

CHAPTER 12: *ELIZABETH*

A thin woman with high cheek bones and long dark graying hair, it seems that Elizabeth's marble-like skin has not seen the sunlight for a long time, if ever. Elizabeth closes her eyes and whispers to Maryam, "I'm not sure I really want to know. But I suppose I need to." She smiles and then folds her hands, as she sits down and somberly watches her life on the monitor.

"Venir Ici!!" the ladies yell out. There is much commotion in the wide hallway. Several women pick up the newborn baby, place her in an elaborately decorated bassinet, and flutter down the long corridor with great fanfare. The sweet melody, *Air De Couer*, plays as she is carried away. Her delicate feather-like body is being floated with several hands choreographically lifting her up and down. Her father, Henry IV, and many others, await her in a very large hall. It is 1602. As her father catches a glimpse of her, he smiles and gently embraces her. Caressing her head, he kisses her on the forehead. Her older brother mills about, eager for a peek at his sister. She is named Elisabeth. And later, she becomes known as Élisabeth de France. Her childhood, along with that of her five siblings, is well-structured, with all the amenities as well as obligations associated with being a princess. When she is eight years old, her father is assassinated outside the Palais du Louvre in Paris. Her brother, with whom she is very close, succeeds him to the throne as King Louis XIII of France. When Elizabeth is 13 years old, her family marries her off to the Prince of Asturias, the future Philip IV of Spain.

Elisabeth first meets her-husband-to-be when she is transported to Pheasant Island, in the Bidosoa river, which marks part of a natural boundary between France and Spain. There, by proxy, Elizabeth becomes the new Princess of Asturias.

In 1621, by the time of the birth of her first child, Elisabeth's husband is King, and she: the Queen of Spain. She is of the mind that her husband has quite a few mistresses, but little can be done about it. She is the well-respected, deeply-loved queen of the country, and knows her place. Rumors swirl around court about her having an affair with a famous poet. The Spanish people love Elisabeth nonetheless. She is beautiful, intelligent, and has all the accoutrements of nobility. She has seven children, the youngest of whom later becomes the Queen of France, the wife of her nephew, Louis XIV. By this time France and Spain had gone at war with each other. At the age of 41, Elisabeth contracts pneumonia, and dies shortly thereafter. Her bloodline has reached the 21st century, all the way to the present King of Spain, Juan Carlos I.

Elizabeth says nothing, but her eyes are wide and her mouth slightly agape. The somber yet kind gentlewoman seems dumbfounded by what she had just learned.

"I knew there was something about her that set her apart from the rest of us!" says Alex, laughing.

"Her bloodline has reached the 21st century, all the way to the present King of Spain, Juan Carlos I." Scottie observes rather sarcastically.

"Come now. We have no differences any longer," Elizabeth shyly assures them. "What royalty feels like, I no longer know." She says almost apologetically. "If somehow I felt more precious than others while on earth, I'm glad I'm rid of that delusion now. I'm among friends and equals, as we all are."

CHAPTER 13: *MARYAM*

Maryam stands up and walks away from the monitor to the window. Her strong jaw bones, coupled with her towering height as a middle-aged black woman, make her seem a formidable and assertive figure. Her skin shimmers under the light. She wrings her hands, and stands stiffly, looking out without moving. She seems ill at ease, and looks away into the sky as the monitor tells her story.

"Mama!" says five-year old Maryam, as she fiddles with a short broomstick spinning it in the air.

"You run on and fetch me that pan!" her mother orders.

A tall white woman, the Mistress of the house, enters the kitchen. "We got to prepare the hog for tonight. The mayor of Atlanta is coming," she says to Maryam's mother.

"What did I say girl? What did I say? No more playing and goofing around! Get me that pan right now, you hear me?" her mother says, whipping a dishtowel in the air at her daughter. "Go on, I say! Get!"

A wide-eyed five-year old Maryam quiets down, looking up at her mother wistfully, almost wanting to hold on to the roundness of her, nestling into her nooks and crannies, and nap.

"Folks ain't gonna wait for you to grow up girl! You got to do this, just like I do," her mother says, as she hikes up her apron, and goes out the back door to the pigpen.

"Oh, the Master is coming!" says the Mistress. "He'll be mightily mad if the hog isn't ready for supper."

They both know that in a few hours, the door of the kitchen will slam open and a white man with rosy cheeks and high boots will step inside, as he always does. Maryam only knows him as "the Master," but her mother once told her that he is her father. Every day, while she washes his feet in the basin, he smiles at her, but he never says a word about being her father, and, on strict instructions from her mother, Maryam never asks either.

As she runs to get the pan, she stumbles over a newspaper with fancy letters and pictures. She kneels down to pick it up and starts to look at all the black squiggles and pictures. She knows that her mother cannot read and neither can she. But Maryam wants to know all she can about the secret codes of language, the fancy letters on the page. She stuffs a page into her dress.

"To the kitchen!" The Mistress slaps her on the back of her head. "You move on now! We ain't got time and this ain't no play room!"

Once in the kitchen, Maryam receives a beating from her mother for being late, too. She runs back into the barn, where she sleeps at night, and whips out the newspaper and gazes at it. She studies it for clues, and tries to unlock the codes of letters and numbers that gave meaning to the page. This isn't the first time she's nicked pages of newspaper to marvel at them at night in the barn stall she calls home. She cuts up the pictures and shares them with her four siblings, her mother, and two other women. She has a whole collection of the newspaper cut outs in her little corner of the barn.

Years go by and Maryam grows tall and thin, her paler skin different from many of her sisters and brothers. By the time she is ten, she learns to care for other children in the household like they are her own. Her mother tells her to stay away from white men, and she sees them leering at her when she is out in the fields. At harvest time, she helps pull cotton alongside her mother. The cotton is the worst, because her fingers bleed from the thorns, and she gets yelled at for bloodying the white froth. She would rather harvest rice anytime. One day, she hears several men talking outside the barn. She peeks through a knothole in the wall and sees three men talking to the Master. Their voices are getting louder and angrier.

"I ain't got any more bushels to give you," the Master says. "You are gonna break me. This is a bad year." A short skinny man with light yellow eyes and a goatee steps forward and yells, "Then I am gonna take those Negroes as my pay!"

The Master says, "That's a mighty high cost, but maybe I'll sit on it a while."

"You're gonna give'em to me," the man says, as he reaches around to his back pocket.

Maryam can see he has nothing in his pocket, but her Master can't. He falls for the bluff, and she wants to yell to him, but is too afraid.

"I can't spare the grown ones, but I'll give you two of the boys. That's the best I can do," her Master says.

"I hear you got a couple of good working girls. Throw in one of them and you've got yourself a deal."

Maryam tries to back up from the hole she'd been peeking out, and moves away from the door. But the man pokes his head in the door and spots her. "That one, the young tall one," he says, pointing to Maryam. "How old is she?"

"Don't know," the Master says.

"She looks old enough," the man with the goatee says.

"But it's no matter because I ain't giving that one. The other girl is worth a lot more," the Master says.

"I'll take just one boy for this girl," the man said.

The Master looked at Maryam, then back to the house. "I reckon that'll have to do," he says.

The man with the goatee hurries towards Maryam and grabs her hand. She tries to resist, and she yells out to her mother, "Momma! Help!"

Her mother steps out the kitchen door, wiping her hands on her pocket rags, and she says, "Sir, whatchyou doin with ma girl?"

"Oh, he's just taking her to town for some work. She'll be back tomorrow," the Master says.

"But you can't take my girl. We need her here. She gonna make a good cook. She knows how to make all kinds of food!" The men look at her and keep talking, shaking hands. The man with the goatee has a tight grip on her arm, and she sees her sisters and brothers peeking out, afraid to come further. She doesn't make a fuss because she's afraid they'll come out and do something stupid, like try to help her, and then the man would want them too. So she stands as tall and strong as she can and she tries not to cry. But her Momma is bowing her head and trying to get the attention of the Master. She pleads to him, begging him, wishing he will hear her. But he ignores her. A man grabs Maryam's arm, and the man with the goatee grabs her other arm, and they throw her in the back of the cart. The men jump on their horses and start off. She thinks about jumping off as her family looks to her, all of them crying, and she sees the Master already walking back to the house.

The dust blows in the air behind her and she starts to cry. Then the cart stops, and she looks to the front, thinking maybe the men have changed their mind. Maybe they decided to be decent folk, but the man with the goatee comes around back with a rope in his hand and he ties her to the boards on the front of the cart. Maryam knows he's no Christian.

"This here is one good and strong girl we got us," the man yells out as they arrive in town. Several white men and women are standing by the cart as they pull in. A round woman walks up, lifts Maryam's arm, and feels her muscles, as if she's buying cattle.

"Fifty bushels," she offers.

"I'll sell for 70 bushels, or no sale," the goatee man says.

"I'll give ya 60," the woman says.

"Sold," the man yells. They leave her tied there in the hot sun, and little children come and point at her. The woman and the goatee man walk off under an overhang, and the woman makes her mark on a chit, and comes back. "Well, let her loose. I ain't getting up there like I'm some slave. I bought and paid for her. You get her to me."

The men untied her and pushed her off the cart, where she fell face-forward into the dirt. The little children laughed, as Maryam got up and wiped off her face.

"Get a move on girl!" the woman orders, as she gets up on her buggy. "Now keep up ya hear?"

Maryam runs after the cart even though she knows she has no choice but to go with the woman. The woman stops in front of a new house, bigger than her Masters, but without her Momma inside. Her new master is a short chubby man. He smiles when he sees her. She works in the kitchen, cooking and scrubbing, until the woman lets her go to bed.

Exhausted from work, the woman tells her to go out to the door behind the pantry, where a closet had been made into a room with just enough space for a broken rope bed, piled with old blankets. Maryam backs herself into the bed, there is so little room. She cries all night. She never sees her mother again.

For four years, she cares for the Master and Mistress's children and manages the bulk of the housework and domestic chores. Inside the house, she is a servant, cook, seamstress, and even a nurse. The Master also owns two other black women, three black men, and two young black boys. She is taller than the boys who are her senior, which comes in handy, because she's the one in charge. She virtually runs the household.

Then one day, the Master arrives in the kitchen and tells her to come with him.

"Where Master? Shall I get my cloak?" she asks.

"Oh, you won't be needing that," he chuckles. They ride in the horse cart to a small barn on the outskirts of Atlanta. He lets her ride up front, because he tells her he doesn't want her insides all bashed around. "I need you all in working order," he says.

They come to a barn, and at first, she thinks he stops just to rest. "Get on in there," he says.

As she enters, she notices that there is a young black man in there.

"Take off your old dirty shirts," the Master says.

Maryam hesitates, but the Master puts his hand on his whip. She begins to cry and wants to run away. But the black man, using both of his hands, holds her down and undresses her. Soon after, after much struggle, the black man manages to insert himself into her. The pain is excruciating. She feels torn from the inside out. The sound of her screams sound like someone else's, muffled, far away, and distant. But she could hear the Master's loud laughter real close. She passes out from the pain, and when she comes to, the black man is gone. But the Master is standing there watching as she bleeds.

"You're gonna stay here for as long as it takes," he says. "I don't want to hear about you leaving, or we'll have to come after you. And you know what happens if you run. After all, you'll just be lying around all day. This is like your little sojourn. Think of it as a happy time" He laughs, turns and leaves, locking the barn doors before he does.

Every day, the Master comes, bringing grits or some leavings from last night's dinner. She can tell who in the house has taken her place by the poor cooking. She wants her old place back more than anything, The young black man comes and rapes her again, and again. Then the Master locks her up and leaves again. The black man looks as sorry as scared. She doesn't blame him. She feels as though her body and mind have numbed to the pain. She soon suspects she is with child, but there is no woman that she can ask or even tell what has happened to her. She feels too shamed by what has happened to her.

Soon she is returned to the Master's house, and she works as she did before. But she no longer smiles or whistles. She no longer feels lost in her work. She feels empty inside, even though inside of her a child grows. When she is ready to give birth, the Mistress and a black midwife come to help, and Maryam delivers a baby boy. She holds him in her arms and cries, so grateful for the beauty that came of all the pain. She cries all night. The baby is as beautiful as the sky and Maryam calls him Sky, for his moods change with the wind. She enjoys every moment that she spends with Sky. By the time he is seven, he is taken away from her. She feels as though a part of her has been plunked, ripped from her body. The part of her that she so dearly loved and cherished suddenly disappears.

Maryam had asked her Mistress questions over the years, and by watching her Mistress read and asking her for hints, Maryam learns to read and write. When they discard the newspapers, she would take them, sneak them into bed and read at night. She begins to read the news of the War.

One day, Maryam sees the Master in her bedroom doorway. He is very distraught. "Everybody will die if those negroes don't stop agitating," he said, yelling and pacing back and forth. Maryam gets up and wraps her robe around her, and draws him into the kitchen to prevent the other slaves from hearing what he was saying. She is afraid of the man, to be sure, as she has been since the day she arrived. He continues to yell and starts to pace around the room. Soon the other slaves are milling about the back, trying to overhear what the commotion is about.

That night, she goes out to the barn to talk to the others about what is happening. They whisper, afraid their master will discover them talking to each other. But that walk to the barn is the first step for Maryam. Soon she becomes the messenger for a group of slaves wanting to flee to the North. They decide the men must go first, so they can join the war against the South.

In May 1863, the Master kicks the barn door open and shouts, "Anyone who wants to stay, let me know now! I want the rest of you out of my house today! Y'all hear?" The rest of the day he drinks in the house, while the slaves gather what little they have, and walk off down the road.

But Maryam has nothing, no worldly belongings to speak of, and has nowhere to go. She is also afraid her son will never find her if he ever returns and she is gone. Besides, much of Atlanta had been recently burnt down during the War. She has no place to go. She chooses to stay and become a servant rather than a slave. Having spent most of her life in the kitchen of the house, Maryam remains the cook and the maid for the household. She follows news of her people's struggle for freedom in the papers.

Her Mistress later evolved into a socialite in the Atlanta area., and she often had high-level officials visiting her home. Over years of listening to the conversations at the dinner table when her Master and Mistress entertained, Maryam learns about the rich lives of the white people in the South, and she longs to be among her own people more every year. When her old Mistress dies of pneumonia, Maryam moves out of the house and starts anew in a rundown room in the south of Atlanta. The only upside of the place is the huge peach garden out back. She continues to work as a maid for the Master, and spends most of her free time reading. She reads the newspapers, and as a reader, quickly becomes the central clearinghouse for information for her black neighbors and friends.

When she is about 42 years old, in January, late at night she is walking back to her room from her work at her old Master's house. That month, the South had experienced a deadly winter that caused all the trees to freeze, and many old people died of exposure. Cold and shivering, Maryam walks briskly down the street, her coat collar raised up around her ears, muffling her from the chill. She can hear little and walks fast. Suddenly, she senses something behind her. Before she can turn around, two black men grab her and pull her down an alley. She struggles but they hit her on the head. She screams but no one hears her. The two men, both drunk and uttering nonsense, rip off her clothes and rape her repeatedly. When she begins to struggle, they beat her. One of the men picks up a brick and swings it at the side of her head. Her head snaps back and her arms go limp. She simply drops. The newspaper in her pocket, the *Atlanta Constitution*, which she had picked up from her Master's house that day fall out. It read in bold cursive letters: "January 29, 1899, Negro Criminality Rampant in Atlanta." She takes her last breath.

Maryam never budges from where she is standing, by the window of the spaceship, just staring at the sky. Elizabeth can see the shimmer of the beads of tears in Maryam's eyes.

CHAPTER 14: *ANDRE*

"Scottie, I'm not sure I want to know," Andre says, as he gets up and nervously paces back and forth in the room.

"You have that right, Andre," Scottie answers, making eye contact with him. "But this will be your only chance. We are informing Team 9 about their lives on Earth for the reasons I outlined. As I said before, we all have histories. But instead of dividing us, they unite us in our humanity. They help us understand. But this is wholly your choice. Knowing is not compulsory."

"Well, since you put it that way, let the show begin!" says Andre, seeming satisfied with the explanation as he sat back down.

"I think that's a good decision, Andre."

The monitor begins:

"Hey, Andrzej, can you sniff the clouds to see if it's going to rain or snow today?!" One of his older sisters would tease, almost meanly while chuckling. The only boy with five older sisters, in this Jewish family outside of what later would become known as Gdansk in Poland, Andre is teased a lot because of his tall yet lanky stature. But he is also loved unconditionally. He is born in 1221. The men in his family are shopkeepers, as his ancestors had been for as long as he can remember. They sell garments and woven fabrics. From early on, Andre learns the trade and excels at it. He is a "natural tradesman," his father has always told him. He spends almost all his time in his family's shop. He also works the loom steadily and more quickly than anyone. He has always been skinny with a wiry build. With a triangular face and a large nose, he stands out even within his own family, and it is not hard for his sisters to poke fun at him. They love him dearly though. He is the only boy and a likable one at that. He helps everyone in the neighborhood. As his father has expected, and is the tradition in his culture, he is to learn the trade from his father and take over the shop after his father passed on.

When he is sixteen, Andre falls in love with a rosy-cheeked girl, whose family lives down the street. A graceful girl, from Andre's extended family, she is a second-cousin of sorts. He would see her everyday as she goes out to get water from the well. They soon got married. By the time he is 24 years old, Andre has three children: two boys and one girl. Around this time, his father has become ill, and Andre has taken over the shop. They live on the second floor right over the shop. Every day, he would walk down the stairs to open the business, and all day his children would run up and down the stairs from the house to the shop and then back to the house. There is always a commotion of sorts in the shop with kids, either coming or going. Even the neighborhood kids, including Andre's kids' cousins would constantly frequent the shop. Andre has a way with children and all the neighborhood kids know that they are welcome in his shop. He always has a variety of candies and mastic chewing gum, to hand out to his young visitors.

It is a stormy fall day, and Andre has just come downstairs to open his shop. He hears one of his daughters, Rozalia, his oldest, running downstairs right after him as she often did. She would run outside and play with the neighborhood children until lunch time. She would then run back inside to go upstairs and help her mother clean and prepare lunch for everyone. It is always Rozalia, who brought lunch downstairs for her dad. This day the rain is coming down hard, slamming the ground, and Andre sees Rozalia drenched in water as she runs around with the neighborhood kids. "I can't stop these rascals from running even in the rain," he thinks to himself.

As Rozalia runs around in the street with her friends, she suddenly slips and falls in an open well. Hearing loud cries from the other children, Andre immediately rushes out and sees people gather around the well. Rain is now pouring down "in sheets," virtually "obscuring his view" of the well and the crowd.[10] He immediately realizes that it is *his* daughter in the well. The crowd drops a rope down the shaft to Rozalia, but she is too far down in the well to grab it as it dangles.

Andre decides to go into the deep well himself. As he slides down with the rope, which he is holding with his hands, he hears her daughter cry out his name: "Tata! Tata!" In the dark hole, Andre listens to the sound of his daughter, and follows its direction, letting the rope go as it is too short. Soon, Andre finds his daughter. She is injured and bleeding. He picks her up with one hand and masterfully scales the wall with the other until he could reach the rope, which is dangling overhead. He then ties the rope around her waist. She is pulled up to safety. They then drop the rope down for Andre to climb up. He grabs the rope and begins to pull himself up. At the same time, he would kick the wall with his feet in order to give him a boost. But because of the heavy rain, the wall of the well has become heavy and slippery. As Andre tries to climb up, suddenly, a large portion of the wall collapses, pouring over his head, The onlookers try to throw down another rope and pull him up, but it is too late. His cry for help is muffled by the thick clay covering his face and body. His wife and his children are watching from above. His body remains buried beneath the rubble.

Everyone on the Spaceship is quiet. "Where is Rozalia now?" Andre yells out melancholically, yet uncontrollably. But having realized that he already knew the answer, he too simply falls silent.

CHAPTER 15: *ALEX*

"I bet Alex was a king or something when he was on Earth," says Andre to Michelle, regaining his composure after listening to his own story.

"No, I bet he was a strict teacher, the kind that students always remember," says Michelle. "You mean the kind that his students feared? right?" Elizabeth quips.

Alex simply smiles and says, "I bet I was the maintenance man for the sewage department!" He laughs so hard that his potbelly jiggles up and down.

"Well, let's have a look, shall we?" Scottie puts his finger to his lips to hush them. The monitor shows two people in a heavily-decorated room, with gilded wall carvings and oversized paintings.

"Whether or not you like it, you are a Russian prince," says Alex's father, an elegant man, wearing an ornate suit, and pacing back and forth while Alex is seated. "I'll be darned. Who knew?" Maryam whispers under her breath.

"But Father, this is1854, the idea of being a prince is old-fashioned. We are in the modern world now."

"You are twelve years old, Pyotr Alexeyevich Kropotkin!." yells out his father with a hoarse angry voice. "You are a prince! You must understand who you are. If you disrespect the royalty, you disrespect your own mother. You disrespect the whole Russian society, your own ancestors. Remember, your mother's father is a decorated Cossack general, a war hero. Your forebears have spilled blood for you. You must honor them. You shall live and die for who you are, and for mother Russia," his father proclaims curtly. "Now I'll hear no more about this." He turns around and abruptly walks out of the room. A male serf closes the door behind him.

Alex shouts at the closed door. "I will not allow anyone to call me a prince any longer!"

Two years later, Alex, a young brash man, has enrolled in the elite Corps of Pages at St. Petersburg.

"In this institution, each of all 150 of you young men is endowed with special rights, reserved for and attached to the Imperial Household." Soon, Alex learns that his "special rights" included abuses and hazing of the pages.

"I resent this so-called imperial life style. I prefer if we lived in a communist system, free, free from the central government, founded on voluntary associations between workers," he writes in his journal. "I am

111

a believer in human evolution. We are not predestined." In his spare time, Alex writes prodigiously. He is not alone in becoming further disillusioned with the Government after the failed Crimean War. Late at nights, he and his fellow pages discuss the embarrassment, which France and Britain, significantly smaller countries, caused Russia.

"You know so much about the world," his friends would often tell him. He continues to read numerous books by European political thinkers. "I am not going to be in the army anymore," he declares to his father. "I am going to study at the university." Alex then quits the army, and enters the university to study mathematics. He also becomes secretary to the geography section of the Russian Geographical Society. Between studying, reading, and his position in the Society, he becomes immersed in intellectual thought and circles. "My dear friends, this is 1872, I can no longer accept my existence as a supporter of royalty, or even supporter of any organized government. I am an anarchist!" Alex proudly announces. His friends in the intellectual circles support him, but warn him that his words and actions can bring him serious trouble.

"This may be 1872, but still the Czar and the palace rules over us with an iron fist" one of his friends tells him. "You need to exercise caution and parsing of your words." But Alex does not stop and continues to agitate against the Tzar.

In 1874, Alex is walking home when men from the Imperial army wrestle him to the ground and take him to prison. "You are a subversive and we know your friends in the Circle of Tchaikovsky. They will all be in trouble."

"I need to do my research, my geographical work!" he tells the prison officials, and his aristocratic background carries enough weight to allow him to continue in that role. His work gives him a much needed respite from the vagaries of prison life, and soon he completes a report on the subject of the Ice Age, arguing that it had taken place in not as distant a past as originally thought.

Right before his trial, however, Alex manages to escape the low security prison, with some help from his friends. Carefully and full of bravado, he tells his friends, who have helped him escape, "let's go to a fancy restaurant to celebrate my freedom!" That night he informs them of his intention to go to Switzerland. He does go indeed, and from Switzerland, he travels to Paris, to launch his own socialist movement.

"I have lived away from Mother Russia for many years now. I have written many books on various subjects, including evolution, political thought, geography and other academic subjects. I have been in jail many times in Russia, and even right here in France," Alex tells a crowd of well-wishers in Paris. "Now, I am going back. The old regime is gone and Bolshevik revolution is closer to my way of thinking. But I am an anarchist nonetheless, and will not join this new government, despite the fact that they have offered me the position of minister of education." The crowd cheers loudly and bodes him farewell back to

Russia. He returned to Russia in 1917, at the time of the Bolshevik revolution.

Shortly, thereafter, in Moscow, he writes: "I am disgusted by what this new government is doing. This buries the revolution. The Bolsheviks are becoming as authoritarian as the Czars were. Nothing has changed. Socialists cannot become autocratic. If they do, sooner or later, the country will turn back to capitalism." Alex prophesizes after the Russian revolution. "I will not accept any position in this new government as it would be against my anarchist principles." Alex tells the press.

"I appeal to the young" Alex writes. "Don't let anyone tell us that we-but a small band-are too weak to attain unto the magnificent end at which we aim."

"I am here today back in Russia because on February 8, 1921, my friend Peter Kropotkin (Alex) a great man, a purely brilliant mind, and a lucid thinker of our times has died of pneumonia. Anarchists around the world have lost a true leader," says Emma Goldman, a famous American anarchist thinker.

The crew on the Spaceship remains speechless, several nodding their heads in approval of Alex. Suddenly, they seem to have developed more respect for Alex. He just sits there, gently stroking his beard.

CHAPTER 16: *PRANAV*

The monitor opens on Pranav's story and the crew is taken aback by the beauty of the scenery.

In 1732, the monsoon season has just ended in the Rajasthan province of India. The lush green trees drip with dew and the heavy steam rises in the air as monkeys call noisily to one another, hanging and jumping from branch to branch.

"This is *my* son. Not yours," says Pranav's grandfather, Maharaja Sawai Jai Singh II, pointing to 5-year old Pranav. He is saying this to his own son, Pranav's father. He had just founded the City of Jaipur. Pranav's father knows better than to argue with his father and lowers his head.

"Pita (father), do you want him to be raised here in Jaipur?" Pranav's father asks.

Pranav's grandfather does not answer, but continues to stroll with his son and his grandson around his large picturesque terrace set on a hill overlooking the City.

"I have just created the first modern Indian city, divided into nine squares and with magnificent buildings around the City," he says, walking back and forth. "This is an epic project. It will take years and years to complete. You have two boys and one girl. I will need Pranav to follow in my footsteps in order to finish the project the way I would have if I were to live to see it completed. You must understand that dear son."

Pranav, a five-year old boy wearing his western shorts, complete with a vest, runs around the Chandra Mahal, a large imposing palace.

"I am not political, you know. I just love India. So you see, we must use the British technical knowledge to our advantage. Beta, come here!" His grandfather calls Pranav, as his son.

7-year old Pranav comes to him. He shows him a drawing of a new tunnel, which his engineers and architects have just completed. The peacocks in the lawn strut about, squawking.

The years go on and Pranav learns and studies the British technical knowledge his grandfather reveres. Pranav loves learning about design, buildings, and science, and he learns quickly. By the time he is ten, Pranav is drawing architectural designs. This is a source of great pride for his grandfather, who never loses the chance to show off his grandson's work to business associates and friends.

"This is Mr. Vidyadar Bhattacharya, the chief architect in the royal court. Now that you are 14 years old, he will become your mentor," his grandfather tells Pranav, as he introduces him to the middle-aged man. "He will teach you what you need to know."

Pranav politely bows to his new teacher. Mr. Bhattacharya says to him, "You will come and stay at our building, which is like a school. You are very fortunate because you will work with me as well as with Sir Samuel Swinton Jacob. Have you heard of him?"

"Of course!" Pranav says, his eyes widening. "He is the very famous engineer who has made everything in India." He exaggerates a bit out of deference to Mr. Bhattacharya, an effort that doesn't go unnoticed by his grandfather.

"I want to learn about everything," Pranav gloats.

"You should study English literature first," his new mentor tells him.

His grandfather has always said that "my Beta will excel in all sciences and academics," and so Pranav feels that he simply must.

For years, Pranav studies dutifully, and by the time he reaches the age of 25, he is called to the city center to receive an honor. Everyone in his family attends the ceremony. His mother and sister make great meals, and their servants work hard to clean and dress up their home for festivities after the ceremony.

"The British Raj of the State of Rajasthan hereby appoints you as a scientist for the City of Jaipur," one of the two British men in military uniform declares. Pranav's grandfather is stooped over a bit with age, but eagerly looks up, beaming with pride. "This is our gift to you on your 25th anniversary of your birth," the other British man

says, approvingly nodding to his parents and grandfather.

After the ceremony, his grandfather takes him aside and tells him,

"Beta, you will have a great opportunity to work with several well-

known scientists. You should be proud and work hard."

"To honor you, I will do my utmost Pita," Pranav says.

Less than a year later: "Now, I give you my daughter to keep and

to have for the rest of your life," says a gentle bearded man. In the

tradition of the Poddars, you will live in a Haveli with your wife."

Pranav smiles and bows in respect. His mother and sister accompany

the bride as they kiss and hug her.

"The Raj has commissioned you to build a tunnel to be constructed

under the City. This tunnel will be 800 meters long and used in case

of an attack," his grandfather tells him. "This is a great honor that you

are now trusted to build a secret tunnel," he whispers.

A year later, he tells his grandfather, "My first child is just born Pita."

"You are excellent in everything you have done, and only 28 years

old. I hope your child will follow your foot steps."

The next day, Pranav leaves the Haveli, which is considerably far

from Jaipur, to go on a field inspection of the tunnel. In the afternoon,

his convoy returns from the inspection, and the group stops at a river

to rest. The heat is sweltering, and the air doesn't move, but the sound

of the strong current beating against the rocks sounds like relief.

"It is very hot. Shall we go for a swim to cool down?" one of the engineers asks.

"It is unbearably hot. I agree," Pranav says. "Let's do that."

Everyone jumps in the flowing river to refresh and cool down. "The current is strong but the water is nicely chilled," Pranav thinks as he takes a dip. As Pranav swims, suddenly one of his feet becomes entangled in the algae at the bottom of the river. He struggles to free himself, and begins to kick up. He slips and loses his balance. The powerful current begins to drag him. He yells for help. Two men close to him try to grab on to him, but as he is being dragged, they cannot risk going too far. Pranav is soon dragged away from everyone else. Worse, some of the men themselves become entangled with algae. Pranav is being pulled under. He is unable to breathe. The current is higher than his head and he comes up for an instant, only to see one of his men also washed away. Desperate, Pranav flails his arms, desperate for something to grab onto, but to no avail. Within minutes, he loses his battle and his body, wrapped in algae, begins to float. Several villagers pull his body from the river almost five kilometers away. His turban, sitting on the bank of the river, bears the medal given him by the British Raj for his recognition as a distinguished scientist.

Pranav is breathing heavily as he watches. He tries to seem calm, yet beads of sweat form on his forehead and begin to fall on his white sleeve.

CHAPTER 17: *WANG*

Wang shyly walks toward the monitor. "So, this is going to show how I died?" she asks impatiently. "I want to know how I lived."

"Well, if you insist!" Scottie says, grinning like a wild cat.

"Your life, like everyone else's on this ship, like everyone else down on Earth or up on Kepler-22 had many ups and downs. Unless you were lucky enough to come to this Earth as a stillborn, which you were not, you can be sure that you did not have a boring life by any stretch of your vivid imagination. A boring life is an oxymoron anyway. It does not exist."

Wang smiles at Scottie's answer, but nods her head, humbly.

The monitor begins.

"Another girl? Why can't you have boys like Lu Ding's wife? She always makes her husband happy," Wang's grandmother complains to her mother.

Wang's mother is used to these kinds of comments from her neighbors and relatives. She simply smiles but says nothing. It is the Year of the Dragon, 1688, and Wang's parents have taken her birth as a good omen. Wang's four older sisters giggle as they carry the newborn Wang in their arms. They almost treat her like a toy. The family lives in a tiny remote village near Harbin, the northern city in China.

"This is a beautiful baby! This is a beautiful baby! This is a beautiful girl who nobody would ever want!" The oldest sister hums playfully. The sisters all laugh, and start to sing along the words, as they walk towards the rice field.

"Bring her back! I need to give her milk! She must be so thirsty from all your tossing around! She is a girl, not a doll!" Wang's mother yells out. The girls laugh as they hurry back towards their mother, who is standing in front of their hut. She snatches the baby from her daughters' arms and runs around the side of the hut to breast-feed her daughter, and she hums a lullaby.

Though it was far away

It stands so clear today

The mountains, pagodas and green waving fields

We were flying on a dragon's back

And spirits surrounded us

The day we touched each others' souls

Before I go to sleep

Renouncement is all that I need

To keep me from having

The same dream again

We were flying on a dragon's back

And spirits surrounded us

The day we touched each others' souls

The rain is falling cold

To me it glows like gold

On roof tops of longing

Were reaching for the stars

We were flying on a dragon's back

And spirits surrounded us

The day we touched each others' souls

Wang is fast asleep. The lullaby works every time. She wriggles and smiles, dreaming her little dreams.

The years have been hard on the fields, with little rain for almost three years. Wang's father comes in the door of their hut. "The field is dry. We need more rain," he says nervously.

6-year Wang runs inside after him. She's already been working in the rice field, alongside her mother and aunt. Her mother follows.

"The rice is too tiny. Not good looking," Wang's mother says.

"You must do something about it!" her father shouts. "If you had told me sooner, I could have dug another well. But I'm too old to dig wells now!" He pushes past Wang and her mother, knocking her mother to the ground, as he stomps out the door. "I will marry someone who can give me boys. I will not die here starving," he says as he storms out.

But he does not leave. For the next ten years, Wang and her mother and her sisters work the fields. The harvest does not improve much.

From early on, Wang would often create unusual shapes while tilling in the rice fields. She would often get scolded for wasting her time while there was so much work to do, her mother and father would tell her. But her mother soon realizes that these shapes could help with irrigation when there was little rain during that season. The shapes neatly designed and carefully sloped by Wang would bring water from low lying areas to the hard-to-reach rice fields, resulting in much healthier rice crops for that year. Everyone in the village thought she was very smart, but given the fact that no one was literate, or had any concept of science, they simply nicknamed her "strange Xiao Wang."

One day, an old man with a mustache comes to the door.

"Are you from the government?" her father asks the man.

"Yes. His highness, the new Qing Emperor has ordered me to collect taxes for the year. You have not paid for so many years now."

The father says, "You can see my fallow rice fields. We have had no rain. And I have five daughters. A man in my position can do nothing. We can barely eat."

The man stands there stroking his mustache, ruminating, looking this way and that. Then he looks at the sisters, all lined up beside their mother, standing in the back of the room. His eyes stop on Wang, and he licks his lips.

"How old is your daughter?" he asks.

"She is old enough to work by herself in the field," her father says. "She may not be so many years old now though. She looks more grown than she is."

The man says, "I have a son who is an ironsmith. He needs to get married.

"Does he have his own shop?" Wang's father quickly asks.

"Who are you to ask me? If I consider taking your daughter off your hands, you should be grateful. But I will tell you so you can pray for their success. He will have his own shop soon, but he needs someone to cook and clean for him, to give him sons."

He looks expectantly at Wang's father, waiting for an answer.

"I will have her ready for a wedding next week," Wang's father says, delighted with his luck.

Three years later, Wang's husband, a bald chubby man who sweats profusely, walks in the hut from his work.

"Where is dinner?" he barks without looking at her.

"I want you to come message my feet," he says just as he has every day since Wang got married to him. She wipes her hands and gathers a wet cloth to wash his feet. She begins to work on the arches of his feet, for they are the least riddled with fungus. He grabs her hair and slaps her in the face.

"I heard you were talking to Lu Wan's wife!" he shouts. "She is no good!" He slaps her across her rosy cheeks again. "I don't want you to talk to her again. Ever! Understand?" He looks Wang sternly in the eyes as he holds her pony tail in his hand. "Answer! Do you understand?"

"Yes," she says, her head hanging down.

"So then, you confess! You have been talking to her! I forbade you and you went against my wishes. She is a cheap whore; everybody in the village knows that!" he yells as he stands and grabs her neck with two hands. He then throws her down and picks up a stick he always keeps in the corner of the room. He begins beating her with it. "You will not talk to her again," he orders.

Wang runs out of the house and into the yard where her husband's relatives, mother and sister are watching. He chases her and kicks her so hard that she flies in the air. She lands face down in a pit and stays there crying. His mother walks up and says, "Now go inside and make him dinner. You have made him so upset."

Although barely able to get up, Wang wants to do as she is told. With her eyelids swollen, and her cheeks bruised, she stares her mother-in-law in the eyes. The world is spinning around her.

"You are childless, infertile, dry, like the desert! He can marry another woman who will bring him a son. You are useless Wang! Useless!" she says as she walks away, leaving Wang lying there.

Wang finally rises and drags herself to the house. Inside her husband is sitting upright, fuming, his arms crossed and his face red, while she cooks his meal. She quietly places the dinner bowls in front of him.

"You are not going to live long if you behave in the way you do," he says to her. "I can kill you and no one will blame me. I know," he continues coldly, as he slurps on the soup.

He then stands up, leaving the empty bowls of rice and soup to go to the other side of the room and sleep on his hard clay kang, as he does everyday. Soon, he is snoring very loudly.

Wang's battered body aches all over. She watches him while he sleeps. Then, she stands up and goes out to the yard. She picks up the farm pitchfork, which she has used for years to in the rice field.

Pitchfork in hand, she walks in the room and moves steadily and quietly toward her husband. The pigs squeal in the pen, as if they can foretell an event.

She stares at him with the form in her hands. She thinks of his daily beatings and the constant yellings. She thinks of the humiliation, the time he broke her nose, her bruised body, the pain, day in and day out. He is snoring even louder. She cannot stand it. She raises the pitchfork, her arms pained with the weight and from the beatings.

Though she's held the pitchfork for years in her hands, her purpose is a heavy one now, and with the full force of all she's known, she lands the pointed three-pronged pitchfork into his chest. He jolts forward, screaming. With terror in his eyes, he looks at the huge blade. Blood gushes out and he cannot breathe. The pitchfork has planted him, pinned him firmly into the clay Kang. He tries to scream but cannot get breath. But the pigs squeal hysterically. She hears the footsteps of his family coming, women and men running towards the door. She just stands there, watching him.

Several men push her aside and try to pry the pitchfork from his chest but it does not budge. By grappling with it, they widen the hole in his chest, which bleeds all down the sides of him. His eyes bulge in fear. Then he stops moving. His large round body jerks violently a few times. And then it stops, only pulsating.

His mother grabs Wang and begins to wildly thrash her.

"You killed my son! You whore! I will kill you. I will destroy you!" she screams as she claws at Wang. The other women join in and Wang falls down on the floor like a limp doll, without will. The men pry her from the midst of wailing women and drag her outside. The villagers gather and the village elders look straight at Wang and one of them says, "You killed Xiao Xin, the Ironsmith! For that, we will kill you."

Wang's hands and feet are bound with bamboo straws, and she is strapped to a barn door in the dark. She is bleeding everywhere. It's a cold moonless night in the rice fields. The weather in the Harbin area can get exceptionally cold.

At midnight, several men walk over to her. She is unstrapped and brought to the center of the village. The men bring in five ropes. They tie a rope around her neck, one on each hand and each leg. She simply watches on as they are weaving the ropes on her. She feels numb and the tight knots do not bother her anymore. The whole village is watching as the cold wind is howling. Five horses are brought forward, and the men tie each end of the rope to the leg of one horse. The horses stand calmly as the crowd looks on. The village elder, stroking his long beard, declares, "You are a murderer, and now you will die."

Wang is afraid, but seems to welcome the end to her suffering. She has no verbal response. The horses are standing with their backs facing Wang. She is in the center of the five horses. She sees the different colors of the horses and notices the white one, the one she once rode. She had often wanted to ride the horse to the ends of the earth, and in a way, she thinks, she will now do exactly that. The horses cannot even see her. Five men with whips in hand stand by the five horses. Standing on a small hill, the old bearded man raises his hand and motions to the men with whips. The men raise their whips and in unison whip the horses. The horses gallop away in five different directions. Wang's body began to tear apart, her head being severed first. The crowd looks on in horror as Wang's body is torn into six parts. Her torso is left in the middle of the village for everyone to see. Her parents, her sisters, are crying and screaming. After an hour or so, most of the crowd scatters and returns home, while her own family remains, sitting on the dirt, wailing.

Wang is visibly uncontrollably shaking as she sits down by the window of the spaceship.

Elizabeth walks up to her and lays her hand on Wang's shoulder. "Don't worry dear, that was your past. It is over now."

"But I was a murderer, I killed someone!" Wang whispers.

"You reacted to your environment my dear. You defended your right to live peacefully, and you died for it," says Scottie. "There was and is so much injustice in the world on Earth. You simply stood up and said that you did not want to take it anymore. That's all."

"Where is he now, my husband, is he up here? Have I seen him?" Wang nervously asks.

"Everyone is on Kepler-22, my dear. Yes, he is there too," Maryam says. "You probably did not come across him because there was no love between you. You are closest to those whom you loved and those who loved you," adds Scottie. "And you see, now you are here with us."

Andre joins in, smiling. "Wang, you know, we are all nice and friendly on Kepler-22."

"I am glad," whispers Wang as she looks up to them all. "I am so glad."

CHAPTER 18: *THE END IS THE BEGINNING*

Within minutes of the De-sexing Ray, as the crew on the spaceship awaited to see the results, some species of bacteria began to die out. Others lived longer. Freddy the rooster lives to the ripe old age of five, while Shaq dies at four after being attacked by a pack of coyotes. Most of the insects, including the bees, die within the first three to four years. In fact, the two bees on the west coast of Africa die within a month. The bearded collies passed away within the first 10 years of the de-sexing, each having lived a full and happy life. Virtually all livestock is dead within five years. Within the first twenty years, most non-human mammals have died off, without having had any offspring. In fact, in the first twenty years, the biggest news everywhere in the world is the absence of any births by animals or human beings.

Many humans still survive after twenty years since the De-sexing Ray hit, but there are no children. The last child was born 19 years ago. The remaining human beings, even the young ones, seem weak. Many look old and frail, and even if they are in their thirties, they seem to be ailing. By age twenty or thirty at most, they begin to experience various types of diseases. Their bones are brittle and their skin is sallow, an unhealthy yellow or pale brown color. This is partly due to the fact that they no longer eat meat or fish because all the animals have died off a long time ago. Nor do many have access to fruits because very few fruit trees have survived in the absence of pollination. Fruits and produce, now made in laboratories, are scarce and when available, are for most, prohibitively expensive.

People wander about aimlessly. They have never become aware as to why this has happened, but they realize they are a dying species, the last generation of humankind.

As the Team 9 crew looks on, they see few happy faces. Tabloids and even mainstream media outlets, run by a few remaining groups are awash with countless rumors of apocalypse and doomsday theories. Conspiracy theorists take to radio and television, claiming this to be the work the government, their own or a foreign one. Many also believe that this is God's punishment for their sins. Others blame the environment, while a few even blame what they consider a no-holds barred sex-crazed society. Virtually no one, however, seems to believe that the destruction is the work of extraterrestrials. This is probably largely because no one has seen any unusual species or activity somehow connected to outer space.

"On average, before the De-sexing Ray, 150,000 people on Earth died per day, which means about 108 deaths per minute," Pranav says.

"There were about 270 new people born every minute. This means that before we de-sexed the planet, every minute about 160 people were added to Earth's population. Now that we have stopped that process, the number of deaths has increased to between 500 to 700 people every minute, while no new people are born. So in about 75 years Earth time, in fact even much sooner, virtually all of them will be dead."

"Remember when we started this de-sexing process, there were about 500,000 people over the age of 100 on Earth," Scottie says. "So, by today, the tenth day by our reckoning since we hit the Earth with the De-sexing Ray, which is equal to 100 years on Earth, 500,000 is the maximum number who could still be alive. But the fact is that because of the lack of food and medical support, all but a few have perished."

Through his telescope, Andre scours the Earth looking for signs of life. The monitors show empty dilapidated streets, full of trash and debris. The conditions look grim indeed.

There are still some old men and women, a few of them centenarians, walking about helplessly. They don't know what is happening. They do not know why they are in this sorry state. With no doctors or nurses, empty hospitals, and no drugs available to them, these people no longer consider themselves lucky to have outlived the others. There is no one left to care for them. Even the viruses and bacteria in these people's bodies are dead or dying and gone. Their bodies can barely survive without any microorganisms. They are in pain and starving.

There is no one to pick fruit and produce. All the domestic animals died off almost 80 years ago. Water is scarce, and if found, is often contaminated with toxic materials. There are no cars, trains, or planes moving about. There is no gas, and no one to fix cars if there was. Buildings and houses are old and dilapidated and in need of major repair. There is no electricity, and the elderly warm themselves by burning old boxes. Every day, more men and women collapse and die. In effect, the world has been catapulted back to the Stone Age within a few decades. Those who have died though are on Kepler-22, awaiting their return to Earth.

A couple walks together, still holding hands. They look very old and frail, but it is hard to tell how old they really are given their bad nutrition for so many decades. The woman looks the man in the eyes, and after witnessing another person collapse, she asks, "What will you do when that happens to me?" She raises her cane and points at the collapsed man.

He has tears in his eyes when he responds, "I will go with you. I must go with you. I won't stay here."

The dying continues, on streets, in beds, and in back alleys. No one buries the bodies. They simply remain where they fall.

As the last few near death, Team 9 watches and waits. The crew anxiously waits for the moment of truth, a moment for which they have been preparing for a long time. Scottie sends signals to Kepler-22 to prepare to send the people who recently died back to Earth. The moment of transition is fast approaching.

The couple, the last two people alive on Earth, hugs each other. The woman looks at her husband, smiles, and closes her eyes. He pulls out a gun, which he has kept with him all these years. He shoots her first, and with weak and trembling hands, shoots himself in the head. This marks the end of humans and humanity as occupiers of Earth.

While clearly moved by these tragic scenes, the crew on the spaceship is equally thrilled that their mission is nearing its end. There is a sense of relief on the Spaceship, and the crew regains focus on the upcoming transition.

When the last human dies, the world goes pitch black. The sky seems to be sucked into a black hole. There is nothing, no sound, no air, no light, no movement. Team 9 watches and waits. The eerie silence is deafening.

Suddenly, a fissure of light appears in the Eastern sky. A bird darts through, and starts to flit about and begins to sing. Then more birds fly through the crack. The blue sky opens up, and a sea of color paints everything on Earth. The color is much deeper and clearer than it has ever been on Earth. This fresh-paint look is everywhere, on the trees, flowers, and oceans. Even the rocks look radiant and pristine. Bees begin to hop from flower to flower. All the living creatures of the last hundred years—the humans, Freddy and Shaq, the dogs, all who have gone to Kepler-22, reappear, as if a computer screen had gone dark and is now simply refreshed. Everyone looks vibrant and healthy although they have the same exact features as they did before they died, except that all the children now look 25 years old. Everything seems serene and breathtakingly majestic.

In Beverly Hills, Brandon opens the door to his house. He walks in and calls, "Honey, I'm home."

Scarlet is standing by the window, looking out, and does not turn around. As she stares at the sky, she simply smiles and whispers, "So am I."

Awed and humbled by the experience, Team 9 heads home.

EPILOGUE 1: *AGING & LIFE ON EARTH AND ON KEPLER-22*

As they head back, Scottie asks Team 9 to gather in the main portal. Everyone but him takes a seat. "Ever wonder why we had to look our age when we came to Kepler-22? Wouldn't it have been more ideal to have had our body also returned to us new and improved? Why aren't we all like these guys (pointing to Andre, Michelle, and Jacob), looking vivacious with smooth skin and rosy cheeks?!"

The crew looks around at each other.

"Well, my friends, sadly, I do not know the answer to that. But I do know how we arrived at looking like we do when we died—some looking old and decrepit like me!" Everyone laughs. He now hops on the platform, the round seat protruding from the wall.

He gazes out the window at the blue planet below and pauses, almost in reverie, before he continues. "On Earth, from its very beginning, everyone and everything aged. Even inanimate objects, such as wood, bricks, cars, and clothes aged. The aging process on Earth was a very interesting phenomenon. When we were human, we took aging for granted. In fact, we accepted it. We thought we should all age and then die. But why would anyone want to sit around and wait to die? For all of us, that is exactly what we did. The fact is that aging is really an illness, a disease—as the Earth scientists called it, a 'pathology.'

"Every day on Earth, about 150,000 men, women, and children died. Many suffered excruciating pain before they did. But for some strange reason, this occurrence happened as a granted reality. In fact, we expected it. Some of us even thought that desiring to live for a long time or to be eternal was somehow abnormal, wrong-thinking, or even selfish."

"So they would rather die instead?" asks Jacob.

"Not 'they,' but 'we.'" Yes, yes, you're correct, my boy." Scottie sighs. "It was akin to a herd of buffaloes when a lion attacked one of them. The rest stood nearby and watched helplessly, even indifferently, until it was their turn to be killed."

"However, from time immemorial, there have been those few who thought otherwise, those who wanted to defy this natural yet unhealthy process."

Alex adds, "There is an ancient myth about the first known person to challenge death. He was called Gilgamesh, the king of the Uruk-Sumerian dynasty in Babylon, the country now called Iraq. Gilgamesh went to the bottom of the sea, the myth goes, and found the tree of life, the plant of eternal youth and longevity. In his time, as the myth goes, he was often described as two-thirds god and one third man. However, he was cheated out of eternal life by a serpent."

"But on a more realistic note, there is a scientific aspect to aging, which lets us understand it better." Pranav observes. "Senescence or biological aging was the change in our biology after we aged and our system matured'.[11] There are a number of theories as to why senescence occurred; for example, some on Earth believed it was programmed by changes in genes, others thought that it was the cumulative damage, which was caused by the biological processes.

"However, the reality is that senescence was not the inevitable fate of all organisms," he continues. "A variety of organisms, including some cold-blooded animals, have negligible senescence. This fact, and recent scientific successes on Earth in rejuvenation and extending the lifespan of some animals such as mice by two and a half times, and some others by as high as ten times, have inspired hope in humans on Earth that aging may similarly be canceled, reversed, or at least significantly delayed. Of course, to be sure, because of what our Team has done, they won't have to worry about that anymore," Pranav grins.

"Aging shows itself through the declining ability to respond to stress, decrease in balance, and increased risk of aging-related diseases. Death is the end result of aging. In other words, aging on Earth was due to the failure of genes maintaining or repairing our molecules."

"So, it was really the genes' fault that we aged on Earth," observes Andre.

"Yes, sort of. But remember that we are so much better off on Kepler-22 despite what happened to us down there," Alex says, as he points to the blue planet. "Although we look exactly the same as we did on Earth, we are all healthy on Kepler-22," says Alex. "So if you were handicapped on Earth, your handicap will be cured on Kepler-22, where you will otherwise look the same, but with no handicap. One other reason also why we no longer age is that we do not have calendars or even a concept of time. Everything flows together seamlessly. There is no year, month, or hour. We always live on the same time plane, kind of living in the present all the time. What Scottie said earlier about 100 years on earth being equal to 10 days on Kepler-22 was simply to use a standard of time used by people from earth. Our focus on Kepler-22 is to get whatever we are doing at that moment done, to accomplish our mission, not simply to get them done by an arbitrary time. We are a goal-oriented species now, not a process-oriented one as we were on Earth. Of course, the fact that we are eternal certainly helps!"

"Yes, we do not believe in the existence of time. We don't say, I'm so many years old. We don't measure our lives, because it is not measurable. We simply believe that we have always been alive, and will be for eternity," Scottie proclaims.

"Also," Scottie adds, "as Elizabeth has mentioned, young humans, children will all become physiologically twenty-five-year-olds by Earth's standards once they are on Kepler-22. So, if you are twenty-five or younger, you will accelerate to age twenty-five and will then be twenty-five for ever, which means there is a special perk for humans who die young. So I guess, Richard Dawson, the Earth's TV actor and showman was right when he said: "to die young, is lucky."

"So, aging does not affect us anymore simply because we are up there on Kepler-22?" Michelle asks.

"On our planet" Elizabeth says, "Kepler-22 that is, all of the people who used to live on Earth are still alive, but they no longer age. They walk about as if they are twenty-five-year olds, even if they look ancient. Their physiological clock has simply stopped. There is no more need for repair or maintenance of molecules or cells. Except for how they look, which is based on their original genetic make-up coupled with their life experiences on Earth, they are all on a par with each other in every sense of the word, no matter when they arrived on the Planet. Their intellect is based on their intellect on Earth, but they all have a common awareness. This awareness is a universal one, not an individualized one. For example, although they may not be aware of what each one of them has done during their time on Earth, even if they have committed unacceptable, unforgivable acts, they now innately have an understanding that those acts were wrong, despite

141

the fact that they don't remember the specifics of the act itself; they subconsciously learn from them, and move on."

"Like you said Scottie, in our world, the concept of time, a primitive concept does not exist." Elizabeth continues. "We all live at the same *time*. Past, present, and future are all on the same plane. It's such a liberating experience. When I speak with my friends who were born tens of thousands of years ago, I do not think of them as ancient, old, or unsophisticated. We have all arrived on Kepler-22, we all now speak the same language, and we are all a million times smarter than when were alive on Earth. For practical purposes, we are treated as equals on our planet."

"And because we are all treated as equals," Maryam interjects. "No one is better or somehow more favored than anyone else. On Kepler-22, Hitler lives side by side with Jesus, Cyrus the Great, Peter the Great, and Attila the Hun. Mary Queen of Scotts does not live a better life than Mary, Jesus's mother, or Elizabeth Taylor for that matter."

She continues, "Some victims interact with their tormentors as if they were the best of friends. Those who were executioners, or even murderers on Earth can be seen walking with those they killed. All is forgotten, but not necessarily forgiven. In a sense, our memories have not been wiped clean. We have evolved and learned to go beyond those memories and relearn how to live. We no longer engage in petty habits such as holding grudges, hatred, or violence. Nor are we slaves to the primitive concepts of redemption, retribution, or punishment. We are far above and in fact beyond that. We don't exercise power over each other. Not one of us can or does order another one to do anything. We don't have to anyway. We simply do what is reasonable and equitable because that is the right thing to do. Our system, our life style works because we all intuitively know what we need to do to coexist with our fellow beings. There is no hierarchy. As long as humans on Earth could exercise power over each other, there were always wars and misery because some of them would realize that they had the opportunity to overwhelm or rule over the other group, and they did. Such conflicts could take place between two individuals as well. Self righteousness is just as dangerous as thugness and violence. In fact, in many ways, they are one and the same."

"On Earth, they were constantly waging war." Scottie jumps in. "They waged wars even when they wanted something good to be done. They called it a "good" war. They waged war against hunger, drugs, even poverty. They even tried to fight illiteracy. It was a very base human response to perceive everything as a fight. They battled cancer only to be confronted with another disease. They attacked viruses and germs. Always attacking, always fighting. But to what end? They have not achieved much with this behavior, this always-on-guard, defensive, or offensive attitude. In the country called America they have a cartoon character called Bugs Bunny..."

"You mean Looney Tunes?" Jacob excitedly interrupts. "I know about that!"

"Yes, something like that. In one of the cartoons, Elmer Fudd, chasing Bugs Bunny ends up shooting at a barrel instead, and then he tries to cover up the holes with his fingers. One hole, then two, then three, and suddenly a hundred! There was no way humans could ever succeed by trying to cover up all the holes in their lives at the same time." Scottie holds up his hands in an ironic gesture.

"And they don't know that?" Asks a perplexed Michelle.

"No, they don't. They were programmed to believe that everything in their lives was a fight, a struggle, and that they should overcome obstacles in whatever way they can," responds Scottie. "We on Kepler-22, in contrast, have learned that we are not separate from each other or even from the environment around us. We and our environment are seamless, a continuum encompassing everyone and everything. We are effectively floating in this environment, navigating through it. There is no fighting with anything or anyone. There are no enemies, nothing adverse. Everything is in motion together, flowing together, working together as part of the same unit. We operate like a school of fish, we move as a unit, and when necessary, maneuver our way around a problem or an obstacle together. But we never stop lest be run over by those problems or obstacles. Instead of fighting a disease, we embrace it and then disarm it. We are not afraid of anything or anyone. In fact, there is no such a thing as fear on our planet. In such an environment, there is nothing or no one to be afraid of. Viruses, which kill so many on Earth, are helpless here because we are not afraid of them. Although they don't exist on our planet, but even if they did, we don't fight them. We disarm them. Our immune systems, in fact, is one that no longer tries to defend anymore— It would coexist with the viruses if they existed on our planet and then it would transform them into friendly ones."

"And we are also free from figurative diseases. We do not fight poverty because there is no reason for poverty. On Earth, humans are the only species that are often ashamed to be poor, even if they can't help it. On Kepler-22, we are alive forever, and there is no concept of possession, there is enough for everyone, and because of that understanding, we do not have to vie for survival, for power. No one dies anyway. Indeed, we have found that the key is to make sure no one has power over anyone else—no one!" Scottie concludes.

Maryam says emphatically and proudly, "As a result, there are no leaders on our planet. For all intents and purposes, in practice, we are all equal, really equal."

"So, how is it that we live forever? Are we not made of the same material as the people on Earth? Then why don't our flesh and bones decay?" Michelle asks.

"Good question. In our world," Pranav explains, "Remember, there are no bacteria or other single-cell organisms on our planet, of the kind, which cause decay and destruction. Our bodies never perish. They continuously regenerate just like a deer's antlers or a hydra's head. This is a non-stop process. God or nature, whatever the Earth people believe, did not make a perfect body for us. We, therefore, do not have much of a choice but to try to make this imperfect body eternal."

"On Earth, in the medical field, there are two sub-fields of what they call biology: gerontology and geriatrics. Both concern aging." Pranav says.

Scottie suddenly jumps back in: "You see, the people on Earth are stuck in a global trance: *they are afraid to live*. There have always been people who believed aging was a disease. Benjamin Franklin, whom you can see walking around on Kepler-22 every day, believed that science would one day *cure* aging. On Earth, you are born, then you are young, and then if you do not die of an accident or one of the countless diseases, you will quickly (within a few decades after age twenty-five), if not sooner, begin to fall apart. By age seventy or eighty, if you are not already dead, your limbs are ready to give way. You move around more slowly for fear of breaking your bones. At this stage, many humans and other animals break limbs that do not heal properly. Shortly thereafter, often within a couple of years, their heart gives way."

"As I've said before," Scottie continues, "death is the end result of aging. When we were on Earth, we always wished, if we were able, like Humpty Dumpty, to put all the pieces together again. Now, that is done on Kepler-22."

"You are right Scottie!" Maryam says. "Humans waste a lot of their time trying to prepare for old age. But at the same time, they don't want to get old! They are always amazed when they find themselves to be fifty, sixty, or seventy," Maryam says. "It lulls them into silence and often depression. 'What happened?' they ask. 'When did I get old?'"

"Like I said, the reason we get old is because our cells decay and die off. Our bodies are made of cells and stuff between the cells," says Pranav. "On Earth, these cells keep dying in all beings. If, instead, these cells regenerated periodically, as do the cells in stags' antlers, people would never grow old, get sick, or die, especially when there is nothing to cause decay like bacteria. In fact, even on Earth, the 'hydra' practically did not age. Some plants on Earth, too, had learned to cheat the system. Take pines, for example. They retained their needles all year round and had adapted to the system."

"If the people on Earth had made discoveries in gerontology, as they were about to before we arrived," warns Scottie, "they would have been able to regenerate cells, which could potentially increase their life span to two hundred or even a thousand years. We did not want that, ladies and gentlemen!" He says, emphatically and sternly. "As a matter of fact, there were some elements, scientists on Earth, one of whom was named Aubrey De Grey, who was actively pursuing this goal. We had to stop him and other people like him. There is simply no room for such a huge population. So far, there are only two planets in the universe that we know of, which can sustain life for humans. One is Kepler-22, which is full already, thanks to Earth people irresponsibly.

EPILOGUE 2: *EARTHLY PERCEPTIONS*

Wang asks, "Why did people on Earth have all these beliefs about God and a creator? Why did they think we have to have a creator? Did *we* also have that when we were down there?"

"Oh, yes, my dear," replies Scottie. "Most of us did. Humans began thinking about these even when they were living in caves. There was a need for an explanation, a solution to all our ills on earth. There was so much confusion and frustration, so much sadness and anger, so much death and misery, so much disappointment. Sometimes this way of thinking even led to mass hysteria. Humans were practically helpless against what they considered Nature or acts of god. People died when they were very young, when they were at the prime of their lives, or even when they were old but not ready to depart. They got sick and had to contend with their sickness, which affected everyone in their families. There were also too many unanswered questions in their lives. That is why they sought refuge in religion and other belief systems. They sought answers and help. Religion seemed to provide them with that."

"But once we departed and came to life on Kepler-22, we realized that the search for a higher being, the search for knowledge, was in vain. We had it all mixed up. We thought that there had to be a humanly explanation for anything and everything. We called this 'knowledge.' But the truth is that there is no knowledge. There is no such a thing as knowledge! Knowledge on Earth is man-made, only for humans' consumption, and by extension, the fruits of such knowledge are also man-made and flawed."

"And also," Elizabeth says, "interestingly, humans were incapable of retaining or transferring even their flawed knowledge on a mass level or often on any level for that matter. They were like their own Olympics runners, who were supposed to pass the torch from one to another. The difference is that every time they tried to pass the torch, it got extinguished before they even changed hands. Even if they tried to pass some of it, knowledge that is, alot got lost or they ended up confused and in fact lost themselves! When this happened, they had to start all over again! There has been an immense amount of so-called knowledge collected over the millennia, but sadly this has not been passed on to most people, and as result, they kept on repeating and making their own mistakes."

"Humans are weird," whispers Andre.

"Yes, we were," Elizabeth comments wisely.

Andre continues to whisper: "They often asked questions without really wanting an answer. Every morning, for instance, they would ask each other, 'How are you?' But they really did not want to hear the answer!"

"On Kepler-22," Elizabeth says, "we have done away with all these so-called niceties, these shallow gestures."

"How about the way they judged each other by the direction of their bodies." Pranav adds.

"What do you mean?" Asks Jacob.

"They called a person a leftist or left-minded or right-winged simply because he or she thought a certain way. Now, I really find that weird." Pranav responds.

"How about what they called "commercials" where paid actors blatantly lied to their audience by seeming happy beyond belief when they drank a simple liquid, only to sell products to the people? How weird is that?" Asks Alex.

"Okay! Okay! But let's not get too carried away. We get the idea. We acted awfully strange when we were down there," says Scottie.

"As for the so-called 'knowledge' of humans, which Elizabeth was talking about," Scottie continues. "Up on Kepler-22, we have collected and preserved what useful knowledge that we could gather from Earth. We have then created a reservoir of actual understanding of the universe, a combination of a collective knowledge of the ages and a collective conscience, if you will, which has become an indelible part of its inhabitants' psyches. It is manifested by our incredible intellect and our intuition. Our people are now smarter because we can all tap into a massive collection of human experience, not just individualized versions of limited knowledge as humans do on Earth. You remember when Carl Sagan, the astrophysicist, died a few years ago, and with him died all that knowledge, which he had acquired? They asked him what would happen to his knowledge when he died of cancer. He wistfully replied, 'I would love to believe that when I die I will live again, that some thinking, feeling, remembering part of me will continue. But as much as I want to believe that, and despite the ancient and worldwide cultural traditions that assert an afterlife, I know of nothing to suggest that it is more than wishful thinking.'[12] Same with Einstein, Avicenna, and all the other noble people. All that hard-earned knowledge and experience, at least a big bulk of it is simply buried in the ground. No more! Now, on Kepler-22 we not only have this cumulative body of past experiences, we also keep getting regularly updated, similar to what computer software does on Earth, the so-called Artificial Intelligence, but a million times faster and more accurate, when new discoveries are made. This way, we no longer make mistakes that were already made by those before us. And history no longer repeats itself."

"Furthermore, on Kepler-22, there is no knowledge of the fabricated type they have on Earth," Scottie declares, following the other Team 9 members' train of thought. "No need for that. On Kepler-22, what the primitive people on Earth considered as knowledge is refined and then has now simply become inherent in us, embedded within our psyche. We continue to call this knowledge for now, as our counterparts on Earth are too primitive to fathom another concept. The universal knowledge on our planet sits at the base of our collective conscience. This knowledge encompasses everything we need to know. It is at least a million times more comprehensive than all of today's encyclopedias and information on the Internet on Earth combined. Also, the difference is that our knowledge is not quantifiable or linear as it is on Earth. We simply *know*."

Scottie points at the trees in a forest on the monitor and says, "For instance, we learned on Earth to call a tree a tree, even though the term is quite an arbitrary one. We identified objects by shape and size, weight, and location, etc., and then gave them names or labels. This way, we could survive in our primitive way, and so we could communicate what we wanted to say to another person. Imagine how hard it would have been to say, 'Go up to that thing sticking out of the surface of the Earth and pick those moon-shaped fiery things'! Instead, we found it easier to say, 'Go up to that tree and pick the red apples.' The same is true with everything else we did. By inventing language, we made the tremendously harsh and difficult life on Earth simpler, more manageable. But no matter how much we tried, because of our insurmountable limitations in our intelligence, and especially due to our inability to communicate clearly, and also because of our inability to intrinsically pass on our knowledge to one another, there were endless problems between countries, between groups, and even between individuals. As a result, there was mass confusion on a cosmic scale."

"Who are we kidding? Living on Earth was hell! Sheer Hell!" Scottie chuckles as he walks away.

Every one of us is, in the cosmic perspective, precious. If a human disagrees with you, let him live. In a hundred billion galaxies, you will not find another.

Carl Sagan

END-NOTES

[1] Marnia Robinson, "Your Brain on Sex" http://www.reuniting.info/science/sex_
     in_the_brain.

[2] Id.

[3] Id.

[4] Id.

[5] Id.

[6] Id.

[7] Id.

[8] Id.

[9] See: En.wikipedia.org/wiki/Estrogen.

[10] Quote by Kate Chopin, the Storm, (1898), taken from Wikipedia, and governed
     by CC-BY-SA.

[11] Some of the content concerning "senescence" came from:
     http://www.princeton.edu/~achaney/tmve/wiki100k/docs/Senescence.html,
     and is governed by CC-BY-SA.

[12] Wiki Quote, governed by CC-BY-SA.

Printed in the United States
By Bookmasters